Longing for Eagle Cove

a small town Oregon romance

by

M. L. Buchman

Discover more by this author at:
www.mlbuchman.com

Cover images:
Man And Woman Holding Hands Walking Photo ©
Geribody | Dreamstime.com
Douglas Fir Tree © Kongxinzhu | Dreamstime.com

Buchman Bookworks

Other works by M. L. Buchman:

Angelo's Hearth
Where Dreams are Born
Where Dreams Reside
Maria's Christmas Table
Where Dreams Unfold
Where Dreams Are Written

Eagle Cove
Return to Eagle Cove
Recipe for Eagle Cove
Longing for Eagle Cove

The Night Stalkers
MAIN FLIGHT
The Night Is Mine
I Own the Dawn
Wait Until Dark
Take Over at Midnight
Light Up the Night
Bring On the Dusk
By Break of Day
WHITE HOUSE HOLIDAY
Daniel's Christmas
Frank's Independence Day
Peter's Christmas
Zachary's Christmas
Roy's Independence Day
AND THE NAVY
Christmas at Steel Beach
Christmas at Peleliu Cove
5E
Target of the Heart
Target Lock on Love

Firehawks
MAIN FLIGHT
Pure Heat
Full Blaze
Hot Point
Flash of Fire
SMOKEJUMPERS
Wildfire at Dawn
Wildfire at Larch Creek
Wildfire on the Skagit

Delta Force
Target Engaged
Heart Strike

Deities Anonymous
Cookbook from Hell: Reheated
Saviors 101

Dead Chef Thrillers
Swap Out!
One Chef!
Two Chef!

SF/F Titles
Nara
Monk's Maze

Chapter 1

*T*his is...*different."* *Natalya Lamont* had been to a number of friends' weddings, but none like this.

"But it is *very* Becky," her mother agreed. That had them both smiling because it was absolutely true.

The double wedding, which appeared to be the first in Eagle Cove's history, held in what had once been Becky's father's cow barn, added an extra layer of merry confusion to the event. The best man for both weddings was the same person—one groom's brother and the other groom's son, as it was to be a father-son double wedding this actually made some form of common sense. Greg's brother Harry was marrying Becky and his father, three years after his wife's death, was also marrying again.

Natalya had come down from Portland to the Oregon Coast for the weekend to help set up and decorate, and it was going to be surprising...surprisingly wonderful.

The reception after the pending ceremonies would make this an even more Becky-esque event. She was a top craft-beer brewer, so there was beer rather than champagne. In addition to being best man twice, Becky had twisted Greg's arm (which hadn't needed much twisting), to cater it. His restaurant had just been named the best on the entire coast, making both the Whale Cove Inn and the Heceta Head Lighthouse Bed & Breakfast rather tiffy, and promise of his food might have helped account for the amazing turnout. But most especially of all, the barn setting that was no longer a barn was completely Becky.

A classic January storm was rattling the Oregon Coast hard with intense winds and curtains of lashing rain. Eagle Cove in mid-winter didn't offer a lot of venues for weddings.

The Grange Hall—which for a while had also doubled as the Unitarian Church (which now held service in The Flicker movie theater)—had recently been converted into dog kennels and a training area for Catbird Service Assistance Dogs. Catbird had offered the use of the training space which was big enough, but since it smelled of wet dog…

Her mom's grand Victorian B&B, commanding the head of the beach, had hosted weddings in the past but couldn't accommodate the scale of Becky's. It seemed as if half the town had turned out for the doubled nuptials today. So maybe the draw was more than Greg's food.

"Doubt if you'd get a dozen people at my wedding," Natalya whispered to her mother as they waited for the first ceremony to begin.

Her mother threw her head back and laughed. Gina Lamont had the best laugh; she always gave in to it completely. The people around them joined in with bright smiles even though they couldn't have heard the conversation. Mom's laugh just did that to people. Natalya had always envied her mother's laugh.

"You'll have more than you think, dear. We'll invite Becky and she'll bring her friends."

"Thanks a lot, Mom."

"That is if you bother to marry one," her mother plowed on completely ignoring Natalya's sarcastic tone. "You know my advice."

She did. Her father, only ever referred to as "That Unholy Disaster," had been gone before Natalya was born and her mother had never remarried. A few months ago a stray comment had made Natalya suspicious enough to ask whether or not they'd ever been married in the first place. Her mother had slyly avoided answering by wielding a fresh batch of her irresistible macadamia nut-chocolate chip muffins.

She turned to ask again now, but at that moment Becky's mom, who was as short, blond, and buxom as the bride, made her way between Natalya and her mother like they were pool table bumpers.

"Sorry," she gasped out and waved a cherry-flavored ChapStick as an excuse before plunging back into the crowded "bride's room."

The main room for the wedding was packed, but the smaller space where the two brides were getting ready was utter mayhem. Natalya and her mom had retreated to the big side-sliding door that opened into the main area just to avoid being trampled by the herd. There was no questioning Becky's power to win people over.

And it *was* her influence.

Harry, her fiancé, was a high school troublemaker only recently returned. The other couple, Peggy and Judge Slater, were quiet fixtures of the community and had been for decades.

But everyone adored Becky.

Her mother too won people's hearts effortlessly. Another gift Natalya had failed to inherit along with the big laugh. It was actually okay with her; Natalya often found the social whirl tiring. She had her good friends, and that was enough for her—except they were all here in Eagle Cove while she lived three hours away in Portland.

In another way, Natalya *had* followed closely in her mother's footsteps, taking a lover when she wanted one and only keeping him until he became boring—which never seemed to take long. But now the second of her two best friends was tying the knot, she was less sure of her choices.

First Jessica and Greg. Now Becky and Harry. That left Natalya and…nobody. She didn't even have anyone to invite as a wedding date, never mind someone with potential for longer term. That wasn't good. But a quick flip through the mental contact list of past affairs also didn't unearth any regrets. Which was good. But it should tell her something…only she couldn't think of what.

However, it was impossible to feel too morose in the glorious mayhem that was a Becky Billings' event. Her friend absolutely knew how to throw a party.

"Aren't they starting yet?" Becky's father came up and asked for the twentieth time in the last ten minutes.

"Check your watch, Max," her mother told him for the twentieth time.

"Oh," he looked at it. "Right." And he was gone again.

"Do you think he actually saw the numbers this time?" Natalya asked.

"Not a chance." Her mom waved at Carl Parker then jabbed a finger in Max's direction. "They'll be talking cows and hogs in seconds."

"No," Natalya shook her head. "The weather." And sure enough, both men turned to look out the nearest window being splashed with rain. They'd been the two big farmers in town before Max Billings had given the farm to Becky and retired to Alaska.

Eventually, the winter venue options had come down to The Flicker movie theater (awkward and nowhere to dance afterward), Peggy's airplane hangar (chilly even with the big heaters running and presently mostly filled with a disassembled 1930s Beechcraft Model 17 Staggerwing that she was restoring), and Becky's barn (so much more inviting than it sounded even before they started dressing it up).

Becky's barn had won the day.

Over the fifteen years since they'd graduated high school together, Becky had converted the cow barn into one of the best craft-beer breweries on the Oregon Coast. The milking stalls had been replaced with a giant copper cooking kettle, massive fermenting tanks, a bottling machine, lines of kegs, and all of the other strange and magical equipment Becky used to practice her art. She'd walled in a part of the upstairs hayloft as an apartment, which was a very cozy space combining bedroom, kitchen, and bath. They'd recently taken over another section of the hayloft for Harry's home office.

The old, ground-floor milk processing room had been converted into their living room. From there Becky could keep an eye on any batches she was brewing. She'd made it into a homey and comfortable space…that was now a whorl of bridal-prep mayhem.

Bridesmaids, best friends, well-meaning wedding guests, and family were all crowded about them in what had been the milk processing room and was now a very comfortable living room.

The wedding proper filled the former calving barn to capacity. Becky had turned it into a tasting room. She'd refinished the inside wood so that the Douglas fir planking glowed warmly under a wash of indirect lighting. A long oak bar took up one end of the big room. It now served as a backdrop for the ceremony.

Behind the bar were lined up a dozen beer taps, from Windy Wheat Ale at one end to Rushing River Stout at the other. And there was always a pony keg of Becky's Original Root Beer hooked up as well, a brew she'd started selling for a dime a bottle back in fourth grade. The taps were all shaped like bluebirds for Becky's childhood nickname, with the flavor clearly marked on each bird's wing.

Above the bar at the far end of the room was a massive painting of the town of Eagle Cove as if seen from a plane flying offshore.

It was one of the best things Natalya had ever worked on. It was also one of the last paintings she'd ever done. Her life in Portland was web and product design, and she'd only picked up her brushes a few times in the years since she'd helped do this.

The town filled the two-mile stretch of beach from the rocky headland of Orca Head with its proud lighthouse to where the

Eagle River arrived after a rushing descent out of the Coast Range mountains into the broad reach of Eagle Bay. The town proper was nestled where beach met bay and backed by the start of the dense state forest that covered the rugged slopes. No town history explained why it was called Eagle *Cove* when there was no cove to be found for miles around.

Natalya wondered how the Judge felt about that painting—and that he'd be married beneath it. It was based upon a photograph taken by his wife-to-be. But it had been painted by his late wife and Natalya. It was one of the last works that Ma Slater managed before the cancer drove her to bed. She'd been such a guiding hand for Natalya's own art. She didn't know about the Judge, but it certainly made her own heart hurt.

Ma had used the detailed style that had made her famous up and down the Oregon Coast to render the town she'd so loved.

Natalya had then painted the framing foreground of massive Douglas fir and coastal pine to the sides. She'd added the three-masted schooner *Wawona* that had transported massive loads of Oregon lumber and fish down to San Francisco in the late-1800s—though getting the perspective and rigging right had almost made her crazy. She'd had much more fun adding the mother-daughter team who had platted the town at that time. They had both been very fashion conscious so it had given Natalya a chance to render them in full Victorian style, her absolute favorite era, though it had been hard to resist steampunking them up a bit. Unwilling to mar the composition with their animosity (history told that they hadn't spoken once in the last forty years that they'd lived in side by side houses) but also not wishing to rewrite history, she had arranged for them to be looking in different directions.

The two women also had been avid birders. So they had divided the town, through intermediaries: the seaside half of the town to have streets named by the mother for land birds and the landward half by the daughter named for seabirds. Hence, the single question that the Eagle Cove Chamber of Commerce received the most often. They'd divided the town's naming right down the middle of Beach Way, Eagle Cove's main street, then moved into the two grand Victorians at the end of town. Natalya and her mother were direct descendants of the daughter and the Slaters had bought the mother's property when she passed.

Natalya wished she'd worn a watch so that *she* could check it. With the bride's father happily catching up with his old friend and neighbor, Natalya was now the one impatient for the first ceremony to begin. Her own antsy feelings didn't extend to the crowd's though. Probably because Becky had the foresight to post Alex her assistant behind the bar. He was busy making sure that everyone had a brew to sip while they were waiting. A beer sounded good at the moment.

She turned to her mom to see if she wanted one, but she was busy catching up with Becky's mother—still clutching her unopened cherry ChapStick.

So much history here. Natalya had to try hard again to shake off the sadness. Eagle Cove was so rich and full; it had a texture and depth like a fine painting…and yet she lived in Portland rendering websites and marketing products.

It's a good job, she reminded herself. *You love your job,* she wished her internal voice had sounded more convincing on that second point. Natalya made her living from techno-retro design. She led a whole team of web and product designers specializing in it at ORTech4U2. Her Victorian division of Oregon Tech For You Too accounted for over a third of website and product designs, both period authentic and steampunk "updated." They were on the verge of breaking into film. It should be exciting, riveting, consuming…well it was certainly the last one. She'd definitely feel the pinch of taking off an extra day tomorrow. Tuesday was going to be hell.

By force of will, she focused back on the room itself.

To the sides of the long beer-tasting/wedding room stood an odd assortment of twenty tables and a hundred chairs that had been borrowed from The Puffin Bay Diner and other places around town. Because Becky had cleared out the cases of bottled beer usually offered for sale, there was plenty of room for the dancing afterward.

But first there were two weddings to manage.

"Which of us is first again?" Her mom turned back as Becky's mother rushed away once more. It wasn't like her mother to be spacy about anything. She was a statuesque redhead with an easiness that Natalya had never managed to even emulate never mind possess. Yet being bridesmaid to Peggy Naron, who had been one of the other long-term single women of the town, had definitely put Mom off her game.

"I'm a bridesmaid first," Natalya reassured her. "See?" she pointed to the Judge standing in front of the bar-soon-to-be-altar. He was an imposing man even without his black magisterial robes. In them today, with his shock of white hair and somber expression, he looked truly grand. If he was there, ready to go, then it was Harry and Becky's ceremony first.

Her first cousin Jessica arrived in a flurry. She instantly started fussing with the gown Natalya was wearing. It was a long black sheath that matched Jessica's—it had become tradition among them for the bridesmaids to wear black as they "mourned" the fall of another of their childhood trio into marriage.

Natalya had wanted to shift over to black steampunk. But Jessica had vetoed that—her own marriage had turned her into some kind of a spoilsport, though she and Becky had still been in favor of the black dresses.

Instead Jessica was now fussing with Natalya's flowers (a beautiful bouquet of yellow winter jasmine and red poinsettia— which Natalya had successfully dubbed as Becky's *Ironman* colors), her hair (dark and worn loose past her shoulders, nothing like Jessica's trendy layer cut—though Natalya was the one stuck living in a big city), and then rearranging where the spaghetti straps crossed on her back. Finally Natalya had to slap at her hands.

"Stop it, Jessica. Is Becky ready?"

In answer, Tiffany—who had eased into the role of wedding manager as quietly as she did everything else—gave them both a light shove from behind and between one breath and the next she and Jessica were headed up the aisle, making way for Becky, the bride. Becky's mother and father had come down from their Alaskan retirement to escort their only child. Becky had needed the steadying hand of both of them, so both parents were currently flanking her as they went up the aisle.

Except there weren't really aisles. Some chairs had been moved to the front by the bar-altar to accommodate the elderly, but it was more a friendly gathering than anything organized. Bride and groom sides were utterly meaningless in the packed house.

"We're like plowshares," Natalya whispered as she and Jessica forged a pathway from the bride in the back to the groom waiting up front. She had to shoo Dawn and Vincent's twin girls out of the way several times because they somehow kept popping up in successive layers of the shifting crowd.

"You're next!" Jessica whispered. Then the last of the crowd fell silent as Becky began walking up the aisle.

Natalya didn't get a chance to tell Jessica just *how* unlikely her being next was, though it did make a certain amount of sense. At least by the process of elimination.

The three of them had been best friends since, well, birth. After today she'd also be the last one to be "cheerfully single" as they had all proclaimed over the years.

But there wasn't a soul on her horizon. There were always men hanging around, but none of them were interesting enough for more than a dalliance.

Was it any surprise? She'd never fit in.

Jessica and Becky were like younger twins of their mothers. Natalya's brunette and dusky skin nothing like her friends, her mother, or the few photos of "That Unholy Disaster."

They both had fathers to walk them down the aisles. Natalya could barely remember her father's name most of the time.

"T.U.D." her mother would say when referring to him until his name might as well be Tud. A missing "r" was always implied by her mother's tone.

There was no more sign of Tud in the crowd than there had been over the last thirty-two years and Natalya didn't miss what she'd never had. Not much anyway. She'd never really dreamed about finding a permanent man in her life, but her friends were planting the idea.

The crowd finally parted enough for Natalya to now see Harry Slater standing at the head of the aisle, vainly trying to catch a glimpse of his wife-to-be. Becky was six inches shorter than Natalya and Jessica's five-ten. She and Jessica shifted together so that their shoulders were brushing, just to make it harder on Harry; the move earned them a pained smile. His brother Greg stood close beside him in his new suit; his eyes were only for his four-months pregnant wife.

"You should be banished," she whispered to Jessica as they neared the head of the aisle.

"Me? Why?"

"Looking too damned happy."

"You'll see," was all the frustrating response that her friend offered as she looked back at Greg all goofy-happy.

Natalya didn't want to see. She wouldn't mind a man someday, but they'd have to be cut out of a different cloth than any man she'd ever dated. But if she hadn't found one in all of Portland, she certainly wasn't going to find one here in Eagle Cove.

Now that the wedding party was all assembled—and Alex had served the last beer from behind the "altar," at least until after the ceremony—it suddenly felt very real. The second of her two best friends was about to be married.

For a moment, Natalya wished there was someone here to look at her the way the groom and his best man-brother were looking at their wife and wife-to-be. The second groomsman was leaning down and chatting with the groom. He towered above both brothers and even the Judge.

Cal Mason Jr. was built on as massive a scale as the suit that actually looked damned sharp on him. Cal was the sort of guy you wouldn't think owned a suit but the charcoal gray three-piece looked amazing. Light-haired and blue-eyed, he could be the twin of his father. He'd crossed six foot in junior high and by the time he and Harry were lead strikers for the Puffin High soccer team, he'd topped out at six-four. He had a Nordic reindeer-herder sized frame more appropriate for football, though Natalya could still recall how agile he'd been as he raced up and down the field. Harry might have thought he'd ruled the games, or that it had been a cooperative effort, but Cal was simply in another league. The problem was that he'd known it—not arrogant perhaps, but still too cocky for her taste.

She could see him joking with Harry, probably being "bar" shallow even though they now stood at an altar. The instant Harry spotted his bride, Cal Jr. might as well have been babbling away on some other planet. *Tough luck, Cal.*

He caught on quickly and began scanning the room. His eyes slid past Natalya with as much recognition as—

He jolted and turned back to look at her. Not Jessica. And not Becky. Definitely her.

She made a point of shifting to a preoccupied expression and looking away as if he didn't exist. At least that was the plan. But Cal's attention had riveted on her and she couldn't ignore her reaction to that familiar smile that spread across his features. In fact, Natalya almost bumped into the groom at the head of the aisle, because she was having trouble looking away from Cal Mason Jr.

Only when Jessica pinched her, rather more sharply than Natalya felt was called for, did she veer to the bride's side. Even the Judge looked at her a little oddly.

# # #

What the hell was up with weddings?

Cal wanted to ask Harry, but he was all busy with responses, vows, and the biggest shit-eating grin ever worn by man. Of course, marrying Becky Billings, it was hard to blame the guy. She was damned cute. Wedding white did absolutely nothing to hide how hot the woman was. It also didn't hurt that her smile was just as ridiculously oversized as Harry's.

After a bit of debate, Harry had chosen Greg to do the actual best man dance, carrying the ring and all that. It was fine with Cal; nice to see the two brothers getting along for a change. He'd have bet that to last mere minutes after Harry had moved back into town, but whenever they started getting out of hand one of their women stepped in and shut it down before it descended into one of the wrestling matches that had been their standard form of communicating. They got along better, so he'd have to admit that was one benefit of marriage. Just an unexpected one.

With nothing much else to do, other than make sure Harry wasn't dumb enough to nerve out at the last moment, Cal had set himself to surveying the crowd.

Not a soul from New Orleans for the groom's side. Man had been a hot-shit lawyer down there for a decade and he didn't even have the decency to invite a cute Creole "hot mama" paralegal for Cal.

As for the townies who'd shown up, Cal knew every one of them and had dated more than a few. He knew Dawn—who'd been a total babe since fifth grade—would give him a dance, but her husband would hog her most of the time—lucky bastard. And the way Greg was looking at Jessica, there wouldn't be much cutting in there either.

But even pretending he didn't already know, there was no question where he was going for the first dance. Which took him back to his original question: What the hell was up with weddings?

He'd known Natalya Lamont since before they'd done the old: if you show me yours, I'll show you mine. They'd been six and they'd both chickened. When they were old enough for that question to take on a whole different meaning it had never come up again. She'd blended into the scenery of Eagle Cove until he'd no longer really seen her.

Oh, his hormones had tracked her whenever she'd crossed a room, her and every other girl of their thirty-four person high school class—a field of just eighteen women. Yet for reasons beyond him, he'd never so much as touched Natalya.

Then today she'd come walking through the brewery crowd with her hair the color of dark chocolate and shiny as a new penny, swept down over her shoulders. And those deep eyes catching the Christmas lights Becky had strung everywhere. If he could ever find someone to explain what it was that happened at weddings, he'd also ask them what was up with grown women and "twinkle lights."

As the bride and groom were doing the "Until death do us part" thing, he had to glance over Greg's head to check out what Natalya had been wearing. Somehow that hadn't even registered as she'd come up the aisle. Just that hair and face and those deep eyes that stared straight back without even blinking. It was unnatural how long that woman could go without blinking; like she was casting a spell or something.

Jessica and Natalya wore long black straight dresses complete with black, paper flower corsages.

He got the joke right away. The death of another life of singlehood. Cute. Damned cute. No, that had described Becky Billings. It even described the sleek and shining blond Jessica. It so didn't cover the long shapely woman with smoke-dark eyes.

Natalya had never looked so…

"You can kiss the bride now, Son," Judge Slater told his eldest and Cal had missed his chance to mess with the ceremony just to tease his best friend by protesting when the call for it was made. But he wasn't low enough to screw with "the moment" for his buddy. That didn't mean he was above trying to tap in on the first dance.

Though, if he *could* arrange to slide onto the floor with Natalya Lamont for the first dance, maybe he'd leave Becky Billings and Harry Slater to themselves.

# # #

Rather than the couple returning down the aisle to cheers and congratulations, there was a marginally pre-orchestrated reshuffling that happened during the generous applause.

Becky gave Natalya a quick hug hard enough to drive all of the breath from her lungs, gave a gentler version to the pregnant Jessica, then laughed and raced back up the aisle. She hiked up her skirts to knee high in her hurry, exposing her favorite bright red cowboy boots. She abandoned her new husband with no more than a wink. Though the kiss she'd left behind at the end of the ceremony had definitely been something to behold. Damn, but Natalya could feel envy about that one.

Jessica gave Natalya a nudge to remind her of their wedding rehearsal move. Right.

The two of them moved aside from the impromptu altar and turned to join the leading edge of the crowd. Their role in Becky's wedding was complete, they were now in the audience for Peggy's.

After carefully not looking at the groom's side of the altar for a long moment, Natalya stole another glance. Every time she'd peeked at the groomsmen, Cal Jr. had been looking at her over the tops of the others' heads. It had unnerved her enough to not join in the happy tears streaming down Jessica's cheeks.

They ended up standing close beside Mrs. Winslow—their second grade teacher. She was a notorious stoic who had taken on the personal responsibility of shaping the youth of Eagle Cove since forever. But even *her* eyes were misty. Natalya had liked to think that she, Jessica, and Becky held a special place in Marjorie Winslow's heart.

"I'm just being hormonal," Jessica wiped at her face with one hand as the other rested on the slight bulge of her waistline that would have been invisible if the dress weren't so clingy.

Mrs. Winslow handed over a handkerchief. "No, Jessica. You, my girl, are turning into a mush. Never would have thought it of you."

Jessica had been a notorious non-crier until she married Greg. Even the harrowing breakups of high school had seemed to slide by her like wind past a seagull on the beach. Natalya kept her tears to herself, except a few times when one of her best friends or her mother stumbled upon her at the wrong moment, but Jessica had none of those. Becky wept at heartfelt commercials on TV, especially ones with the puppies and the Clydesdales.

Jessica dabbed at her eyes and for a moment rested her cheek on the shorter woman's gray hair. "I never would have thought it myself."

"Wimp," Natalya whispered.

"You, Natalya Lamont," Mrs. Winslow had that you're-about-to-be-sent-to-sit-in-the-corner look. "We shall wait until marriage and pregnancy happens to you. I think that shall be very interesting."

"Not likely." And for perhaps the first time in her life, that answer didn't sit well. Her mother was the embodiment of how joyous a single woman could be...but that sat equally uncomfortably at the moment.

Searching for a distraction from wedding-goofy women and Cal's constant attention, she found one at the bar-turned-altar. The newly married Harry Slater stepped up to his father and Natalya was still close enough to hear him.

"Okay, Dad. Hand them over."

The Judge actually looked worried. It was a look Natalya had never seen on his face before. Ever. She'd seen brief bouts of fear when his wife had been dying three years before, but never worry.

Natalya started to look away to see where Cal Jr. was, in order to make sure that he wasn't still staring at her, when Jessica nudged her in the ribs.

"What?"

Jessica just nodded back toward the altar.

Harry actually held his father's hand in a two-handed clasp, a degree of closeness that was still very unusual to see between the two men who'd been estranged for so long.

"You'll do fine, Dad. It's me I'm worried about. What if I screw this up?" He made it funny. Something he and Becky shared, always having the right thing to say in just the right tone to put others at ease. It was another skill she envied, and didn't possess even a shade of.

"Son," the Judge's voice rumbled out, carrying easily to where Natalya stood despite the rising chatter of the crowd anxious for the second ceremony. "You'll do fine. Weddings are one of the very best parts of being a judge."

"Then hand them over," Harry repeated himself and plucked at his father's robe. "Pops!"

Judge Slater had served over thirty years on the county bench before retiring to cook at the local diner and hold lawyer's office hours here in Eagle Cove when needed. Harry had just been elected to his father's former judicial seat in November and was now fully instated.

The room slowly fell silent as Judge John Slater removed his robes and helped Judge Harry Slater don and settle them. The passing of the mantle, literally.

Until three months ago, Harry had barely come home in the fourteen years since leaving for college. It was like looking into a new reality to watch the two of them interact at all. That they were exchanging roles—the father officiating the son's wedding and now the son officiating his father's—meant that somewhere along the way the space-time reality in which Eagle Cove existed had shifted.

Natalya felt momentarily lightheaded. So much so that she briefly wondered if, when she drove back to Portland Monday evening, the city would still be there or had the whole world changed along with Eagle Cove.

When Judge Harry Slater was dressed to Judge John Slater's satisfaction, the two men embraced. Natalya glanced aside and saw she wasn't the only one sniffling this time. Marjorie Winslow and Jessica leaned against each other for support and others were doing the same.

"Now, get over there," Harry gave his father a gentle shove until the Judge—for that would always be the elder's name—was standing where Harry had been just moments before. Cal Sr., almost as big as his son and nearly as imposing as the Judge, came up to shake his hand and thump him on the shoulder. Greg shook his father's hand as well before he and Cal Sr. stepped into the bridegrooms' positions.

"He is a good boy," Mrs. Winslow declared quietly.

"You didn't always think so. You never liked Greg," Jessica complained to her old mentor.

"You have brought out a new and good side to that boy. His brother was even worse as a child, but Becky appears to have done him some good, too."

And they all three turned to look at Harry, now standing tall in his magisterial robes. He noticed their attention and he waggled his eyebrows and shot them a smug grin.

"Or perhaps not," Mrs. Winslow said in her driest tone.

Harry looked quite discomfited when the three of them burst out laughing.

Someone started the music and Harry did his best to compose his expression, then he looked up the aisle and jolted as if he'd been electrocuted just like the time Natalya had wired his chair to a hidden car battery in tenth grade science class.

Natalya turned to look back down the aisle. This time it was her mother and Becky who were "plowing" the aisle clear for the bride and the two judges were both rapt.

Natalya couldn't see Peggy in her wedding white except as a flurry of curly dark red hair just visible over Becky's head.

But she could most certainly see Cal Mason Jr. across the aisle. He'd eased back against the far wall so that he wouldn't block others' view of the ceremony. He slouched comfortably there as if he was dressed in jeans and t-shirt rather than a three-piece suit.

But he wasn't watching the ceremony.

He wasn't watching Becky, still in her wedding white, nor Natalya's mother, looking like she was ready to gather up a whole crowd of men with her statuesque figure. Her mother had liked the bridesmaids' slinky-black-mourning-dress idea, but between a knockout figure and short hem, she also looked like one of those classic redheaded Italian models in it.

But Cal wasn't watching Gina Lamont either, though most other men were.

And he wasn't watching Peggy, standing as bride, who barely reached the groom's shoulder when she finally stood beside him. Peggy did look every inch of the woman she was—one who built and flew planes, had climbed the highest mountains on all seven continents, and won transoceanic sailboat races.

Cal Jr. was watching her. Natalya. He wasn't staring, not exactly, but neither was he looking aside. If she had to label his expression it might be…confusion? She wanted to go over and shake him and shout, "What are you looking at?"

# # #

Cal didn't have a goddamn clue how Natalya had got her hooks in him. She hadn't even done anything.

He tried to recall the stick that the girl had been, growing up like a weed before she…grew out. Always overshadowed by her friends.

It wasn't that Natalya Lamont was some sort of weakfish—even as a girl she'd had a spine made out of steel. It even showed in her dancer's posture, so poised that she made everyone else appear to be slouching just a little. Too bad Frau Schmidt, the only decent dance teacher for thirty miles around, had died when Natalya was still a kid or she might have really become something.

No, it wasn't that she was overshadowed.

It was more as if her two friends were such amazing distractors.

Becky was just so out there, a whirling dervish of energy and ideas. She'd started brewing and selling root beer while they were still in grade school. Now she was a hell of a craft-beer brewer. Focused and as ambitious as hell. Once she'd set her sights on Harry Slater, Cal's best friend hadn't stood a chance.

Since birth, Jessica was always blond, elegant, and so damned smart. She'd been able to speak her words as well as write them and always won every argument. He remembered class debates in social studies where she'd pick the crappy side of the argument, yet so dazzle everyone with her words that her team was inevitably the winner. She used to start arguments just so she could win them.

Natalya had always been the quiet one. But not shy kind of quiet. It had taken him a long time, and some bitter experiences that now made him smile even if they hadn't then, to understand that she was the hidden ringleader of the Terrifying Trio. The three of them were always in trouble—no, they always *were* trouble. And any man watching would swear that it was Jessica's or Becky's doing, Natalya just along for the ride.

Unless you caught her quiet smile. She didn't need to brag or show off to others, but she did love stirring things up.

Like the last soccer game of senior year, his final time ever on the field and everyone had known it. Most of the town had turned out, they'd never had such a winning season. He'd long since announced that he was joining his dad in the family bakery straight out of school—didn't need some fancy degree to enjoy himself—though he'd been bummed to have no chance at college soccer.

For that final game, he and Harry had decided that the Eagle Cove Pufflings were going to go out victors even if they had to kill the other team. That it was against their archrivals from just down the coast, the Siuslaw Vikings, would make it all the more satisfying. Then the Terrifying Trio had arrived in homemade cheerleader outfits so goddamn cute and skimpy that it was impossible to look away. However, they had made their costumes up as Viking maidens complete with fake fur and horned helmets and were cheering for the other side. It was so messed up—and classic Natalya. No thanks to them, the good-guy Pufflings had won…in overtime…barely.

Well, Natalya was sure stirring up some things for him. Not just memories, but definite ideas.

There was a roar from the crowd and he blinked. He'd missed Harry doing his first official gig as judge, which was too bad; would have been fun to give him some shit about it later. Maybe he would anyway, though maybe not.

It was cool seeing the Judge unwind enough to lean down and kiss Peggy in public—even if they were…older. The Judge didn't go quite as far as Harry and Becky—making a man wonder if they were going to do it right there on the altar—but he did a fair job of kissing the bride and it was just a little uncomfortable, like the time he'd caught his dad necking with Melanie Andriessen in the back of her own movie theater. It had been long after Mom had flaked and run off with that Corvallis stockbroker but it had still been weird. He knew sex wasn't just for young people—he hoped to god that wasn't the case—but it didn't mean that he wanted to think about it either.

It had taken Cal years to understand why his dad had told Cal's mom to go to hell when she'd tried to come back two months later. It had taken Cal even longer to forgive him. But as far as Cal knew, his mother had gone and done just that, all the way to hell. No birthday or Christmas cards, squat. Damned bitch! No wonder his dad had never remarried. Women were good for only one—

# # #

"Who are you so pissed at?"

Natalya might have resisted Cal's attention.

But oddly, his inattention had been what finally dragged her through the doubly celebrating crowd and across the room. She'd watched him change right through the ceremonies.

First, during Becky's wedding to Harry, he'd watched her with a very clear and, she'd ultimately decided, flattering interest. Then there'd been the puzzled gaze through Peggy marrying the Judge.

It had shifted abruptly afterward. She'd felt a chill as his deep blue eyes had gone ice-cold. Rather than joining the happy congratulations flowing to the two new couples, she'd become aware of the January storm lashing against the barn's tin roof so hard it might have been hail. The two windows that Cal leaned between were dark with the late afternoon and rain streaming down the glass in thick rivulets. She shivered in her thin dress as she stood before him.

"Guess I'm not fit for man or beast," he continued to glower down at her. She should have worn heels. His six added inches of height seemed a long way at the moment. She wasn't used to looking so far up at a man.

"Since when is that news, Mason? You look like some demon god, glowering here in the shadows."

It earned her a bark of laughter, "Well, at least I'm consistent."

That made her smile in turn. She'd forgotten about the drawing. After one of her inevitable teenaged clashes with her mother—back when she'd still cared about not having a father—she'd stormed off into the woods with her sketchpad. She was always doodling in her notebooks and on napkins.

This time, she'd started drawing the Demon Mother, Destroyer of All Hopes, when Cal had come sauntering by in that way he had. She'd started first with the drawing's background, filling it in with the darkness worthy of Rodin's *Gates of Hell* and Michael Jackson's *Thriller.*

"What you at *now*, Gnat?" He'd called her that since kindergarten, like she was the one who was an annoying bug.

She'd slashed her pen, a dozen quick strokes to fill in the demon's face and slathering jaws with Cal's face rather than her mother's.

He'd looked down and, somehow judging her mood perfectly, had said, "Damn! I *am* handsome." Which had oddly cheered her up.

And he was handsome. Even pissed at the world, Cal Mason Jr. dressed up in a snappy suit was a very fine sight—a very tall one, but remarkably fine.

"So," she looked up at him and batted her eyelids, "are you going to ask me?"

"What?" He blinked at the sudden shift in topic.

She'd thought he was sharper than that.

Then his smile shifted and she realized that his thoughts had gone somewhere she'd never intended.

"Dance, Mason. Are you going to ask me to dance?"

"Shit, Gnat, I've just been waiting for all the goddamn weddings to finish to ask you."

And before she could even draw breath, he pushed himself off the wall. He didn't lead her out onto the dance floor, there was no transitional moment to catch up with his mercurial change from demon to lecher to dashing groomsman. Cal simply swept her into his arms and between one heartbeat and the next, they were dancing.

Stairway to Heaven, much to her mother's distress, had come back into style and Becky and Peggy had agreed on it for their combined first-dance music. Natalya had resisted the urge to save a copy of AC/DC's *Highway to Hell* or Mozart's *Requiem Mass in D Minor* with the *Stairway to Heaven* filename onto the playlist because she'd actually looked forward to watching the two new couples dance. Becky had been so happy and she was one of those people who completely deserved every good thing that came her way. Like Gina's laugh, it was something Natalya deeply envied and wished for herself.

She thought to glance around and see just who was dancing, but Cal's mood was a little manic and he bore careful watching. His shoulders were also broad enough that he thoroughly blocked a wide range of sightlines.

"You need to always wear slinky black, Gnat."

"Only for your funeral, Mason." Because wearing it for the weddings had clearly been a mistake. Cal's hands felt as if they were on her bare skin, even though they were merely at her waist. Next time she'd wear a parka…with a bulletproof vest under it. She didn't quite remember sliding her hands up around his neck, even if it was appropriate for the slow dance rhythm.

"Aww. Didn't know you cared enough to come to my funeral. I'll start a guest list."

"Invite Becky. She always draws a crowd." Natalya wasn't very happy with the way that tone had come out.

"I thought I was the one in a grumpy mood, Natalya."

"Don't do that."

"Do what?"

"Call me by my real name."

Cal didn't ask or pry. He just offered a brief squeeze where his hands had somehow wrapped around her back. "Sure thing, Gnat."

She didn't know why it bothered her. She and Cal had never been close. With a graduating class of just thirty-four there had been some point or other where everyone had been friends…or enemies, and it did make for a certain degree of connection no matter what.

But Cal had been outside that norm. They'd never dated, rarely even danced together at the various high school parties (which she was rapidly learning was a mistake, he was a good dancer). He'd never really ticked her off, especially not with the skill that his best friend Harry Slater—correct that, *Judge* Harry Slater—had done, but then the younger Harry had ticked off almost everyone and done it frequently.

More than once, Cal's apparent unawareness of her had made him the target of one of her schemes. Like the time she'd discovered clear casting resin, and rather than embedding a small flower or shell in the clear plastic had encased all of his schoolbooks in it before returning them to his locker. Though she hadn't been able to bring herself to do that to his prized letterman's jacket which had been the original idea.

Her connection to Cal was that he'd always been there at significantly odd moments of her life. Like that day in the woods. Or today when the second of her two best friends became married, forcing her into the unmarried minority. Then he would pop up in her awareness and nudge her out of whatever mood with a joke or a sly tease.

"Say something funny, Cal." Natalya rested her head on his shoulder and enjoyed the way he held her so close yet so carefully. She felt she was floating along the floor as if they were the only dancers.

#

Say something funny? And said in a whispery sigh of a voice close by his ear. It was so unlike Natalya and about the sexiest damn thing he'd ever heard. Who the hell was she kidding?

Cal knew he'd held women this closely, but he couldn't remember when or who. They were dancing as if their bodies were one. His arms wrapped around her until her ribs on opposite sides lay beneath his fingers. Her chest against his… Her head on his shoulder with her nose brushing against his neck… The slightest tip of his head brought her thick wash of hair against his cheek…

This was definitely *not* a time for humor. This was a time for heaving a woman over his shoulder and dragging her back to his cave.

He guided her past Harry and Becky. Harry didn't glance up for a second, but Becky interrupted her bridal ecstasy long enough to stare at him, or rather to stare at him dancing with Natalya.

He mouthed a, *What?*

Becky just shook her head like she was trying to shake off a hallucination and kept an eye on them as her infatuated and oblivious husband spun her away.

Greg and Jessica actually stopped dancing to look at them. Greg was smiling his ass off. He pantomimed like he was catching a bouquet and sniffing the flowers with a goofy smile.

Cal was so not "next."

Jessica's eyes narrowed as she watched them, for a moment looking almost as dangerous as Natalya did.

Say something funny?

"How about surreal?" he finally whispered when he was clear of Jessica's baleful inspection.

"Sure," again in that slow, throaty whisper. What the hell *was* it with women and weddings? How had he ended up dancing with the most dangerous woman here—most dangerous one in Eagle Cove for that matter?

"My dad. Your mom."

"What about them?" A lazy mumble that was more fitting as an invitation for morning-after sex than a dance floor.

"They're dancing almost as close together as we are."

Natalya raised her head sharply. She caught his chin with the top of her head and clacked his teeth together hard on his tongue.

"Ow, shit!"

"Sorry," she went up on her toes and kissed the point of his chin. "All better now."

Which it absolutely wasn't. His tongue was throbbing with serious pain signals, sharp enough that he'd barely had time to be aware of how her soft and warm lips felt against his skin.

She was looking for her mom, but in the wrong direction.

"To your left."

He managed to keep his chin clear as she twisted to look the other way, but her motion left him with his face buried in her hair. It smelled as if it had been clean washed by the ocean air. That's when he realized that had always been her smell. Not the sea salt and seaweed of the beach, but standing atop the rocky cliffs of Orca Head at the base of the big lighthouse. Ten thousand miles of fresh-scrubbed Pacific Ocean air and you were the first person to breathe it since Japan.

That was Natalya. Impossibly fresh. Impossibly alive in his arms. It made him—

"What the hell?" Gnat sounded pissed. That whispery sigh that had him thinking of a soft bed and a naked woman beneath him was gone. Cal felt a bit of sadness; he hoped that he'd get to hear it again. Soon. He'd have to work on that.

He brushed his nose through her hair, slowing for an extra moment to enjoy himself, as he turned to face in the same direction she was. He could see their parents over Dawn and Vincent's heads. It took a moment for them to dance aside and reveal a really clear view.

Gina Lamont wore a black dress as slinky as her daughter's, except flirtatiously short rather than elegantly long. And in three-inch heels that she definitely still had the legs for. It also made her almost as tall as his dad's six-two. She and Cal Sr. didn't quite cling together, though there was little air between them.

Gina's head was thrown back in one of her infectious laughs, her shoulder-length red hair dancing about as if it too was laughing.

Dad was…smiling. He wasn't a grumpy man, but his smiles weren't exactly the most common thing around Eagle Cove.

In sixth grade he and Gnat had once had a class project together—bird spotting. They'd spent a long cold March week getting up early and staying out late, working to make sure they had the longest species list of their class. They'd even kept a tally of how many times they saw each breed. Natalya had an artist's handwriting, whereas he had a doctor's, so she'd written up their final list in count-of-sightings order. The paper had come back with a "90" on it rather than the "100" he felt they deserved, below Harry's "95" too, which really sucked. The last item on the list was circled in red and a "–10" slashed next to it. Gnat had added a final entry to the species without his knowledge: "Cal Mason Sr.'s smiles. Count: 0."

Gnat had dubbed him "The Master of the Dead-Pan Expression," which had stuck among Cal Jr.'s friends for years.

"Hey Cal. Heard that The Master of the Dead-Pan Expression kicked your ass out fishing on Saturday." His dad's salmon had weighed half-again what Cal's had, so it was hard to deny. And his father hadn't so much as smiled in triumph to lord it over his son so that Cal could be angry about it.

Then Gina Lamont leaned in and kissed his dad. It wasn't some friendly peck; it was a joyous smack of lips that his dad appeared to enjoy thoroughly before the Judge and his new bride Peggy swung into the foreground and blocked the view. The kiss was a surprise, but other than the instinctive "Eww!" factor of grown parents having such thoughts, it didn't bother him any.

He turned his attention back to Natalya. He eased her close again, moving them in the opposite direction through the crowd as he could feel her attention still wasn't where he wanted it to be.

She slowly came round.

Chapter 2

What was it with weddings?

Natalya lay in the dark and wondered how the hell she'd ended up here. For there was no question where "here" was—not with Cal's arm draped lazily across her in the monstrous California King bed.

She'd never actually done this at a wedding: jumped into bed with a groomsman. Once or twice with a wedding guest, but only when he'd been particularly charming.

Cal hadn't been charming, he'd been…Cal. They'd danced, shared a beer, danced some more. They'd switched off with Greg and Jessica once and Harry and Becky another time—the five-four of Becky with six-four of Cal had their whole group laughing.

Much to Natalya's surprise, Tiffany had taken a turn with Cal as well. She was an odd, quiet woman who had hacked a farm out of the Coast Range forest a mile past the lighthouse. It had taken a long time before she'd started coming to the twice-weekly knitting groups and coming into town to sell her fresh produce and meats—mostly to Greg for the high-end restaurant he ran on weekends out of the Judge's diner.

Tiffany had orchestrated the two weddings with hardly a word spoken, and done it well. Not much taller than Becky, she could only clasp her arms around Cal's waist as he reached down over her shoulders to rest his hands on the back of her long brown hair.

As Natalya had watched them, she could feel the warmth of the way Cal held her so close. She'd gone eagerly back into his arms for the last dance. And that had somehow crawled into her brain…or her brain had shut down all together. Because it was a brainless maneuver to land in his bed.

No, actually. The way she felt at the moment, it hadn't been brainless at all. Neither of them had been good for much. They'd danced until the last dance, past eleven, then helped clean up so that Becky wouldn't face a disaster in the morning.

Cal had made multiple runs in his bakery truck to return the borrowed chairs and tables to the bakery and the diner. Rather than closing the Puffin Bay Diner while on his honeymoon, the Judge had arranged for Greg to cover for him starting tomorrow morning, so they had to put it back together tonight.

Jessica and Natalya had cleaned and swept and gathered empty bottles, glasses, and plates until were both staggering with exhaustion.

But when she'd been done and ready to leave, her mother was already gone, clearly forgetting that they had carpooled here. How she was supposed to get back to her mom's B&B way on the far side of town in a bridesmaid's dress on a cold winter night?

That's when she'd spotted Cal. He'd been leaning on a door jamb. Shed of his suit coat and tie, and with the top couple buttons of his dress shirt undone, he'd looked a little dangerous. He'd been watching her intently with his dark blue eyes.

"Hey, Cal," was the most intelligent greeting she could muster at that late hour.

"Coming home with me, Gnat?" He'd asked it so casually as if it didn't matter at all. In a fit of pique she'd simply slipped her arm around his elbow and nodded that she was.

They hadn't even done anything. He'd showered first and been asleep by the time she was done though she hadn't taken long. She should have backed away, gone home, or at least gone in search of a couch to sleep on. It wouldn't be a big search.

He lived above the bakery on Beach Way in the heart of the town. It was a big comfortable space. A great room with a bedroom to either side. The set of steps climbed into the middle of the U-shaped layout and they'd passed through the living-dining-kitchen room on their way to the master bedroom.

She could have gone through the door and slept on the couch.

If only he hadn't looked so nice in the shadowed bed. And he'd folded down the covers on the near side and even been thoughtful enough to set one of his t-shirts there all folded up. A shiver as the storm continued to batter the coast had her tugging on the t-shirt. It was big enough that the neck could almost slip over both shoulders and it reached down past mid-thigh, longer than many of her dresses. The material was warm and thick—thicker than the sheath dress she'd worn to the wedding anyway. Taking a deep breath, she'd ducked into the inviting bed and been asleep in moments.

She didn't know how long she'd slept—amazed that she'd slept at all—when Cal had rolled and wrapped his arm over her as if she'd always been there.

And now she was wide awake, in the middle of the night, and her body was buzzing. So much so, that she was amazed it didn't electro-shock Cal to life. Well, she'd be damned if she was going to lie here like this in his bed. Her mother was always telling her to seize the moment. This time she'd follow that advice rather than slipping away.

She turned beneath Cal's arm, thankful for the protective feel of his oversized t-shirt, and faced him. It was only as she slipped her arm over him that she realized Cal slept without a t-shirt. She tentatively slipped her hand down to his waist—nor underwear. It must be some kind of guy thing, as if showing off. "Hey world, check this out." She'd sleep safe inside her t-shirt, thank you very much…except that it was Cal's.

Natalya was about to chicken out, pride be damned, and slip from the bed when Cal slowly nuzzled his face between her breasts with a low, "Mmmm." Suddenly his t-shirt didn't feel so thick and protective.

"You're supposed to kiss a woman before you do that." They hadn't even kissed last night. She'd simply come home like a… besotted bridesmaid. Besotted by a handsome man who had held her so close while they danced, and gone out of his way to make it clear that it was *her* he wanted to be dancing with.

"Mmmm," he mumbled into her cleavage. "Give me a moment on that." And he tightened his arm around her keeping her in place.

Well, she had brought it on herself. Besides, it was nice to hold a man close. His hair, which was so short it should have been prickly, was fine and soft beneath her hands. She hooked a leg over his hip and let the arch of her foot ride up and down his calf muscle.

"Mmmm," Cal was sounding more awake as his hand slipped down over her hip and cupped her behind.

It was—

A high-pitched tone blasted from his bedside nightstand.

A synthesizer note whistled up and down the scale piercing right through her skull.

Cal didn't even flinch; he continued holding her tightly. He did mumble a brief, "Aw shit!" between her breasts.

Natalya covered her ears as the Beach Boys started singing *Wild Honey.* "What the hell, Cal? Can you stop that?"

"Only if I'm willing to let go of you," she could barely hear him.

"Why is it playing?" She tried to reach out herself but the bed was too big and he had her very thoroughly pinned.

"Alarm clock. Four a.m. Baker's hours. I start early. Need time for dough to rise."

"*Wild honey?*" She echoed the Beach Boys as they hit the refrain hard. "Four a.m.?" She never got up at four a.m.

"Honey. Common ingredient in baking. Part of my alarm playlist. Random foodie hits." He still hadn't let her go or raised his head. His voice was a buzz against her sternum, nose to chest.

"How long do we have?"

"Eight minutes."

"Eight—" she'd never set an alarm only eight minutes before anything in her life.

"I could stretch that a few minutes," he squeezed her bottom suggestively.

"I'm not here for some quickie, Mason." She grabbed his pillow and clamped it over her head to block out the whining synthesizer and over-orchestrated track.

He sighed and held onto her through two stanzas and the final refrain before he pulled his head up. She could feel him squinting at her in the dark and eased back off the pillow as the song thankfully ended.

It would really help if he didn't feel so good.

"Why *are* you here, Gnat?"

"I—" But she didn't have a good answer.

"Not that I'm complaining."

Then a blast of trumpets, a big band intro, and the Andrews Sisters broke in with *Hold Tight, Hold Tight (Want Some Sea Food Mama)*.

"Maybe I shouldn't have asked."

"I—" Again she stalled not knowing what was around the next turn. "Not for a quickie," she went back to her original premise.

"Not what you deserve anyway." He rolled away and slapped at the off button just moments before the Andrews Sisters were going to make Natalya kill herself with an oyster shucking knife.

"What *do* I deserve?" That's a question she'd like answered… in a couple of different areas of her life. Work wasn't satisfying any more—busy but not satisfying. If it ever had been. She hadn't had a decent lover in far too long. And she missed Eagle Cove, Portland was three long hours away. What she "deserved" wasn't even on the radar.

Cal rolled to his edge of the bed and flicked on the bedside lamp.

Natalya was about to cover her face with the pillow again to stop the stabbing light, but Cal had continued his roll and was now parading stark naked around the foot of the bed headed for the bathroom. He'd lost none of the grace that he used to display on the soccer field. Come to think of it, on the dance floor as well. It had been so natural that she hadn't given it a thought as she'd followed his lead, thoroughly enjoying herself in the hands of a skilled dancer.

Over the years he'd also added some muscle, some very nice muscle. Wrestling great quantities of dough every day had given him powerful arms and shoulders. His legs said that he lived on his feet, and the view from behind as he crossed into the bathroom was very nice. Then, in plain view, he planted his feet apart and began to pee. At least he lifted the toilet seat first, but he needed to learn when to close a damned door.

She dragged the pillow back over her face and groaned. This had to be the craziest situation she'd ever been in.

He clomped back into the room. Bracing herself, she went for another peek but had waited too long. He'd already dragged on a black t-shirt, underwear (tighty whities that clung particularly nicely to him), and then slid up jeans.

"It's four now. I get breakfast at six at the diner if you'd like to join me." He dug a set of keys out of his pocket and dropped one on the dresser. "That's for the Vette if you want to get back to your mom's." Even asleep on his feet, he'd remembered that this had all started because her car was at the B&B.

"You'd let me drive your Corvette?" She'd lusted madly for the car the moment he'd held the door for her last night and she'd climbed in. Somewhere in the last six months he'd traded in his practical, red beater pickup for that amazing machine—probably his best friend Harry's fault for returning from New Orleans driving a BMW SLK roadster. The Vette was old enough to be affordable without having become a classic yet; a gorgeous piece of muscle car that had made Natalya feel like a total hot-rodder's babe for the lazy mile drive from Becky's.

"Huh!" Cal looked down at the key, then looked up at her with some surprise. "Yeah, I seem to be willing to do that for you. Nobody but me has ever driven her, so treat her nice."

Natalya sat up in bed, but kept his pillow over her chest in addition to his t-shirt. "Nice? Hell, Cal. I'm going to kidnap it and take it home with me. I'm going to name her Priscilla. You can have my MINI Cooper."

"Yeah, like I'd fit in that tiny thing. And if you try to name her Priscilla, I'm taking back the key." But he left it and started out the door. "Would really like to see you at breakfast," then he was gone.

Nice of him to say, but there was still no kiss. No hug. No second attempt to talk her into a fast romp. What was wrong with him?

Knowing she wouldn't get back to sleep—it felt too strange being in a man's bed who wasn't her lover—she too climbed out. All she had was her black wedding dress and rain jacket. Cal's wardrobe didn't offer any more likely options. He wasn't fat, at all, anywhere, as he'd just proved by strutting about naked as a jaybird, but she could practically go camping using a pair of his pants as a tent.

She peeled up the t-shirt but it was so big and sloppy that she got it all snarled around her head and arms, and hooked over her elbows.

The door crashed open.

She bit off a yelp of surprise and managed to find a hole in the tangle to peek out of.

"Forgot my music player." Cal walked across the room, unplugged it from the nightstand, rammed it into the back pocket of his jeans, crossed back, and closed the door behind him. She could hear him clomping back down the stairs.

What the hell?

# # #

Cal made it five steps down the stairs when the vision slammed into him. He stopped so quickly that he almost tumbled the rest of the way to the bakery. He had to clamp a hand onto the wooden handrail to save himself.

Natalya Lamont, stark naked from the shoulders down.

He'd thought that the wedding dress was so sleek on her that there couldn't be any surprises. Stupid assumption. There were famous movie stars who didn't look half as good out of their clothes. Her dusky skin traveled all of the way down to her toes. Her breasts were goddamned magnificent—not overly big, just full and perfect for her slender frame. And her hips said "Here is a Woman"—with a giant capital W. She had runner's legs that also fired his imagination about how they'd feel wrapped around him as he—

Cal looked back up at the closed door at the head of the landing. Not much to see as he hadn't bothered turning on the lights. It was just an old, wood-paneled hall with a battered front door at the small landing.

Natalya Lamont stood up there, behind that door, naked next to his rumpled bed.

The bakery lay the opposite direction at the foot of the stairs.

He'd had his face buried between those firm, soft breasts… and done nothing.

His body leaned upstairs while some cursed, overly responsible part of him that should still be fast asleep continued downward.

He had held her not for sex but just because she had felt so perfect against him. But the part of him that desperately wanted more of that wasn't in sufficient control to turn him around.

So, he trudged downward and with each step he could only conjure one thought:

Coffee.

Coffee.

Coffee.

He'd thought there was no better way to wake up than between a woman's breasts, but between Natalya's just made it even better. Too bad he wasn't awake yet.

He really, really, really needed coffee. Coffee. Coffee.

Chapter 3

N*atalya slipped quietly out* the side door at the base of the landing, the one that didn't lead into the bakery. She could hear the distant rattle of pans through the wall, but there was no way in hell she was facing Cal at the moment.

The heat on her face should be enough to light up the night despite running a cool washcloth over it. She didn't know whether the fiery blush that wouldn't go away was at being caught naked, his non-reaction, or imagining him standing naked himself in the bathroom while she changed in there with the door closed and locked. And another thing, he may have raised the toilet seat, but he hadn't put it back down when he was through, which evoked memories of both his nonchalant attitude and his magnificent—

Nope! She wasn't going to be thinking about that either.

She floundered through a couple of puddles on the driveway, which her dancing shoes discovered by instantly filling with ice cold water. She made it into the doorless garage where the Corvette was parked next to a small white delivery van with Blackbird Bakery emblazoned in bold letters down the side, with four-and-twenty blackbirds fluttering about. Natalya stood at the passenger-side door for a long moment wavering with exhaustion before she remembered that Cal wasn't going to be coming by to hold the door open like the gentleman he wasn't.

She was more tired than she thought. Four a.m. for god's sake, was it any surprise? She circled to the driver's side.

For one thing a gentleman would have kissed her before taking her to bed, and he'd have stayed awake until she'd joined him there. For a third, he'd have had the decency to say something complimentary about catching her naked—even just an "Excuse me" of embarrassment. But no, nothing. Or he'd at least have put the toilet seat back down.

Climbing into Cal's Corvette was like climbing into…Cal. The cockpit—they actually called it a cockpit he'd informed her last night—was deeply luxurious and surprisingly big. It felt that way partly because Cal had the seat about eighty feet back from the pedals. She scooted it well forward—then decided that she'd leave it there when she returned the car. Maybe she'd stick around long enough to see how he dealt with adversity. He was only six inches taller; by where he'd had the seat, he must drive with the tips of his toes.

Her MINI Cooper was small, spunky, and she'd purchased the sport version so it moved very nicely when goosed. The Corvette rumbled to life with a low throb that barely touched her in the deep leather bucket seat.

She reversed out onto the alley, checking clearances very carefully as she went. She'd wager that even the slightest damage to his precious car would eradicate any chance of a dalliance. That's assuming that she was still interested in having one.

It was an interesting question, even at four in the morning on a drizzly Monday in January. If it had been anyone other than Cal, there wouldn't have been a question—an absolute and emphatic "Bring it on!"

But with Cal there was history, even if it was a lack of history. He was a friend even if he wasn't a former lover. Or perhaps he was a friend because he wasn't a former lover. She loved Eagle Cove, but it wasn't where she lived. She liked the purity of the experience when she came home to visit. Her mother's welcoming hugs and bedding down together if all of the rooms in the B&B were full. They'd talk the night away like lifelong girlfriends. And with Jessica's return, her two best high school friends were here in town as well.

If she did let Cal take her to bed…

Natalya suppressed a sigh.

If she did let Cal take her to bed and they actually *did* anything, she'd have to face him when it was over. If they'd made love last night, it would have been uncomplicated post-wedding sex. But now, it would be something more. There'd have to be planning and a mutual agreement that that was what they both wanted and…

And if she sat in this car any longer in the dark, Cal would find her asleep in the alley.

After a brief struggle with unfamiliar controls, she found the windshield wiper. Clutch, first gear, and she eased down the alley. The Corvette felt like a rocket ship begging to be unleashed, but she only let it idle down the narrow lane, veering to avoid lined-up trash bins and muddy potholes.

Out on the main drag, she opened it up to about ten miles an hour. Its engine climbed to a dull, aching roar before she found the shifter and the clutch in the dark. She found second and the purr shifted back to a mellow throb that a lion might make the moment before it pounced on an antelope. She wondered just how fast this car would go.

In the rearview mirror, which she also adjusted and wasn't going to move back, the only light she could see on Beach Way was the bakery. Nobody else in town would be up for at least another hour; not until the Judge came in to prepare the Puffin Diner for its six a.m. opening. Except the Judge had just gotten married last night. So it would be Greg.

She turned right on LBB Lane. Little Brown Bird Lane dipped down toward the ocean before turning south and heading toward Orca Head and the Lamont B&B.

She went for third gear and the car whimpered about her going twenty on a one-lane road when the car wanted to go a hundred. Why did Cal even own a machine like this? From Becky's and the airport to the B&B was three miles: the two opposite corners of town. It was a town fit for MINI Coopers and scooters—most people walked everywhere on the nicer days. Though January wasn't big on nicer days at the moment.

About a mile out, she spotted a car coming toward town. Unable to imagine who it might be at this hour, she scooted over as far as she could. She recognized Cal Sr.'s beater pickup truck—he was a Dodge man and it was always fun to watch when a Ford or Chevy fan made the mistake of trying to correct his "uninformed" ways.

It was only as he pulled slowly by her that Natalya knew if she recognized his truck, he would certainly recognize his son's car. He offered her a very startled expression during the brief moment their driver windows passed one another. Startled and none too happy about it.

Great. She'd done nothing but sleep and now she'd ticked off Cal Mason Sr. What repercussions that was going to have she was definitely too tired to think about.

She eased the car up to the B&B as quietly as she could despite all of its throbbing and grumbling. The back porch light was on, which was unusual, and the kitchen light as well. Her mother was a creature of habit on one account: she was never, ever up and about before 6 a.m. Breakfast at the Lamont B&B was served hot at seven, warm at eight, and put away at nine.

Natalya managed to park beside her MINI and shut down Cal's "machine"—it hardly seemed right to call it a car. She squished up the steps in her sodden flats and discovered her mother at the kitchen table. It was a small table with a pair of bench seats. It could squeeze four, but had been perfect for a family of two. Natalya had spent endless hours looking out the now-dark window at the thick forest of Douglas fir and spruce while she painted, drew, and even occasionally did homework.

"Mom?" Only the light above the stove was on, so the shadows were thick about the kitchen. Gina sat at the table with a mug of hot chocolate and a croissant. She wore her winter bathrobe of thick, dark green terrycloth and her fluffy white sheep slippers with black noses, floopy ears, and black button eyes.

"Natalya. Are you up late or early? Water's still hot."

Natalya crossed to the stove and debated between hot chocolate and coffee. Hot chocolate meant warmth, comfort, and she'd be headed to bed—her bed. To sleep alone. Coffee would mean that she was going for the jolt of caffeine so that she could stay awake long enough to meet up with Cal for breakfast at six at the diner. Or maybe she should opt for green tea and let her body decide which way it wanted to go.

Wimp!

Never one to turn away from a challenge, Natalya fished out a packet of the gourmet instant coffee, Italian Roast, and poured the water over it. There was only half a cupful in the kettle. She could make more water or drink it like espresso which would mean… And if she waffled on one more decision this morning, she was going to hate herself.

She carried the half full mug over to the table and sat down across from her mom.

"I'm not sure," she tried to answer her mother's question. "I think I'm up early."

"Not me," her mother's smile went a little wicked. "I'm up late. Still have time for a couple hours sleep before I have to start breakfast. Only three guests at the moment so it shouldn't be a problem."

"You and—" Now she knew exactly where Cal Sr. had been, though that didn't shed any light on his perplexed and irritated expression as they'd passed each other on the road. Unless it wasn't about her and he just didn't like being caught.

"Absolutely! I'd forgotten what a good dancer he is. Both on the dance floor and—"

"I don't need to hear it, Mom." Natalya took a sip of her warm sludge-like brew and could imagine she felt the concentrated caffeine bite into her system.

"You always were private about such things," her mom brushed her fingers through her tousled red hair. "Certainly didn't get that from me."

"Maybe I got it from Tud."

"Not damn likely. Oh, your father was pretty enough, ever so pretty. And hands that could—"

"Mom!"

"Sorry. He was a complete hedonist. Made me look like you in comparison. Of course what Cal Mason Sr. can do with *his* hands—"

Natalya groaned…loudly.

"Yum!" was her mother's conclusion as she grinned over her hot chocolate. "So tell me about your Cal."

"My Cal? He's not mine."

"Then maybe I shouldn't ask where you've been the last four hours or why his Corvette is now parked in the driveway," she nodded out the window.

"I— We— He and I— We fell asleep, damn it!"

"Seems like a waste of a perfectly good wedding to me. Maybe if you'd had sex you wouldn't be in such a contrary mood."

Natalya didn't even bother to answer. If she'd had sex, her body would be loose, her emotions mellow, and she wouldn't be winding herself up about leaving in an hour and a half to meet Cal for breakfast. He hadn't invited her back to his apartment for breakfast. Again it had been that casual, *don't really care if you're naked* attitude of his. *I get breakfast at six at the diner if you'd like to join me,* he'd said, without so much as a suggestive leer implying that he was just after a quick tumble.

Her mom's oversized yawn and loose-limbed stretch weren't helping matters.

"Are you going to see him again?" Natalya went for a subject change. "Or was it just post-wedding sex and you're done with him." Exactly as she'd been with every man while Natalya was growing up.

"It wasn't post-wedding sex; it was *great* post-wedding sex. Sure. We live in the same town. I'll probably see him this afternoon as I'm running low on sourdough bread," her smile was teasing as she purposely misinterpreted Natalya's question then climbed out of the seat.

"Seriously, Mom."

"Seriously?" She filled her mug with tap water and left it in the sink. "I can't particularly see why I would. He didn't ask when he left either. Just gave me a kiss and a very friendly squeeze, then went on his way."

Simple sex. Even with an old friend. Why couldn't she have had something like that?

"But Natalya," her mother came over and wrapped her arms around Natalya's head and shoulders and pulled her into a tight hug. "You shouldn't be planning your life by my standards. Your father may have been That Unholy Disaster, but he gave me you and that was worth everything to me. That's all I care about."

Then her mom was gone and Natalya was left with a quarter cup of cooling sludge in the semi-darkness.

For lack of a clearer decision, she knocked it back, left the mug in the sink beside her mother's, and headed upstairs for a shower and fresh clothes.

# # #

Cal had all of the bread dough rising and had started building the pastries when he heard the back door open and close.

Natalya had driven away before he'd even finished the morning rounds. He liked the daily ritual of preparing the bakery. Starting the first pot of coffee. Firing up the glass-doored ovens that his father had installed in *his* father's bakery, which lit off with a low wump of gas. One of these days he was going to put in a wood-fired oven, but it would require a complete renovation to fit it in, maybe even knock out a wall and he wasn't ready to face that.

While the coffee brewed, he had circled out to the front of the house. Here the steel kitchen with its thick rubber mats on red tile flooring gave way to worn oak hardwood that dated back to when his third-great grandfather had built the bakery. He flicked on just one light out in the seating and customer area that would warm the windows for anyone passing by. A glance showed that everything was in place—he'd made sure of that when he brought the loaners back from the wedding.

The wedding.

He'd closed his eyes for a moment and imagined Natalya once more in his arms. Neither t-shirt clad and snuggled close nor mostly naked in his bedroom, but rather sweeping across the dance floor in his arms, swaying to the music as if caught in a kind breeze.

And if he didn't get some coffee soon, he'd sway one time too many and crash to the floor.

Back in the kitchen, he had plugged in his player and kicked off his baking playlist. Unlike his alarm music, it emphasized rock and roll—some his, a lot of his father's. They'd always baked to rock and his dad's taste for the classics had become his own. At the moment Pat Benatar was cranking out that *Love Is a Battlefield,* which Cal rather felt defeated the whole point. Love was supposed to be better than that, though he hadn't given the matter a whole lot of thought.

He hadn't heard the car's return over the music, but the jolt of her arrival had him spraying a smear of raspberry filling over a half-dozen Danish, utterly ruining them, and a long splat right across the stainless steel prep table. He wouldn't even be able to scrape that up and use it because he'd had cornmeal spread down the table for kneading out some rolls that the Brass Plover Inn had ordered to go with their lunchtime chili.

He looked up. "You're—"—not Natalya.

"Morning, Junior."

Cal tried to reply, but nothing much came out.

His dad looked down at the Danish. "Guess you were hoping someone was bringing your Vette back. You know she took it, right?"

Cal nodded.

"Just checking. Driving it like a girl."

"Well, she is one," he finally found his voice. "What are you doing here?" Dad was off on Mondays and the only early mornings he worked any more were Cal's day off on Saturdays. Cal opened the other five days. The shop was closed Sundays.

"Found myself awake. Thought I'd lend a hand."

Benatar finished rocking out and declared her victory.

Dad looked down at the mess Cal had made of the prep table. Rather than scowling, all he did was smile to himself.

Blake Lewis cranked up his beat-box cover of Bon Jovi, declaring *You Give Love a Bad Name.*

"What are you doing up at this hour?"

His dad's smile didn't change. "Just enjoying life, boy." Then he turned up the music blocking further conversation, poured himself some coffee, and they both got to work.

The next couple hours flew by in an easy rhythm. Cal had started working in the Blackbird Bakery when Mom had bolted during third grade. After that, the school bus had dropped him off here just as the bakery closed at two. He'd learned clean-up tasks really well. By high school he was doing prep with his dad for a couple hours before school every morning and worked most Saturdays—except when there was a soccer game. When he went full-time, they'd conferred and added a lunch menu. Simple at first, but over time they'd added homemade soups and hot sandwiches.

But it wasn't until this moment that he missed all of those mornings working side by side with his dad. They never spoke much, not unless Cal was getting in trouble—often Harry's fault back before he'd taken off to be a New Orleans lawyer. But Junior and Senior side by side pounding down and shaping long lines of bread loaves was a happy memory and now a good moment.

If Cal ever wanted to do this with his own son, he'd have to stop goofing around and find himself—

A glance at the clock showed straight up six. He was usually at the diner's door at six sharp to grab breakfast.

"Shit!" He had his apron half off before he stopped. They were in the middle of bagel prep. His father's help had thrown off his timing. He normally had everything quietly rising or baking while he ate his breakfast. But they were ahead this morning. It was also mid-winter on the coast, so it was a much smaller bake than a summer tourist weekend.

"You worried about breakfast?" Senior asked him in between the verses of Boston singing about it being *More Than a Feeling*.

"Not just."

"Maybe worried about your Vette?"

"Kinda." At least about whether or not the woman driving it had come back into town.

"Well go, boy. I got this."

There was something about his dad's smile that Cal wasn't going to hang around and ask about. Come to think of it, he'd been damned cheerful, for him. Especially considering how late they'd all danced last night and how early it still was this morning.

His dad noticed his hesitation and shouted out over Boston's rocking drum riff, "If you're going, go!"

Cal went.

The storm was back, but Cal's jacket was all the way up the stairs and he wasn't going to waste the time. While Cal wasn't soaked, he was definitely cold and wet by the time he'd crossed the street from the Blackbird and hustled down three doors to the Puffin Diner. He bolted up the steps, but stumbled to a halt at the big glass doors.

The diner was empty except for Hector Jackson; Cal was usually second in and Hector was already at his corner table working on *The Oregonian* newspaper's daily crossword. Cal could see Greg back in the kitchen and Jessica leaning against the big steel opening that separated it from the dining area. The dozen tables that Cal had helped Greg move back from the wedding were all neatly arranged without a soul at them. The six stools along the counter were vacant as well.

No Natalya. He felt bad about leaving during the bagel prep. He fought off a shiver. Maybe he should just return to the bakery and—

"Will you quit blocking the door? It's cold out here." A hand shoved lightly at his back and warmth spread from that point of contact.

"Hey, Gnat. Just waiting for you." Without looking back at her, not wanting to reveal his smile of relief, he pulled open the front door. At first he'd thought to hold it wide with a doorman-style bow to usher her through. Then he thought better of it and stepped through himself and, as a tease, didn't hold the door by reaching back until she could grab it.

The spring, strong against the winds that ripped along the coast, slammed the door shut on his heels.

"Hey, Jess. Harry," he waved as the bell on the back of the door tinkled sharply when Natalya yanked it open. He moved up to his normal spot at the counter, dropped down on the stool, and called out, "The usual."

An apparition in a sopping raincoat, citified and stylish enough in a hot blue to completely evoke Natalya's sexiness, came to a stop beside him.

"You've got the manners of a moose, Mason."

He turned to her, primed to offer some pithy comparison himself, but she took his damned breath away. Even angry, and her cheeks and nose scattered with raindrops, she was absolutely breathtaking. In a struggle not to let her know, he shrugged. Before he could come up with something appropriate, Jessica cut him off.

"Tell me something we don't already know. Becky was worried that Cal would drag Harry into his old ways after he moved back." She winked at Cal to show it was just a tease, so he winked back.

But there was a problem there. His best friend was back, but it was all somehow different now.

Harry had been one of the stars of the Eagle Cove Pufflings soccer team. In high school they'd been inseparable, often in trouble with Dad, but inseparable even then. Harry hadn't been close to his own dad, especially not with the Judge commuting up to Newport every day. But Cal Senior made no bones about teaching them both his strict former U.S. Marine Corps moral codes on every topic from girls to drunk driving to girls to drugs to girls. He and Harry had double-dated, gotten drunk, played video games, conquered the soccer field, and played poker together. They'd also never driven drunk, done drugs, or failed to use protection with a girl—Cal Senior had given them each their first box of supply after first delivering one of his lectures.

Then, after bailing for a decade, Harry had come back for one of his infamous twenty-four hour visits, stayed two weeks, and then moved back from New Orleans—leaving what was like the ultimate party town—to become a judge and marry Becky Billings. It just wasn't right. Had they even gotten drunk together once since Harry had come back? If so, Cal couldn't pin it down. Hell, had *he* gotten drunk himself in that time? Shit! When had he stopped having fun and become responsible? He'd better get over that and get over it soon.

Jessica slid across a menu, but Natalya waved it off. The Judge offered a very limited selection and Natalya was local enough to know it by heart.

"Omelette with green pepper and onion and an English muffin." No need to specify the meat, Greg would either be serving bacon or sausage, depending on which Carl Parker had delivered fresh from his farm. And hash browns were not an option. They were a fixture, even with Cal's tall stack of pancakes.

"Coffee?"

Natalya shuddered. "Hot chocolate. No whip."

He'd thought she liked coffee. He couldn't start his day without it. If two people couldn't even agree that the planet was fueled by coffee…

Dumb, Mason. Real dumb. There wasn't anything between them except a bit of wedding night lust. Of course, having held someone as hot as Natalya once, he felt a definite need to do it again. Soon.

He'd start with peeling her out of that raincoat.

He focused on his coffee.

How in the world did a woman manage to look sexy in a wet raincoat?

# # #

"So, what is the queen of the night doing up at this hour?" Jessica slid over a cutlery set wrapped in a napkin along with her cocoa.

Natalya glanced sideways at Cal, but didn't have a good answer. Her design team in Portland started their day at nine only under duress. They had enough East Coast clients where it was already noon, that they had to. But she still preferred working at night and often did—they all did.

Six a.m. was an hour always safely buried somewhere deep in her REM state. Add in the blast of thick, lukewarm coffee at the B&B and her system didn't know whether to panic or shut down, leaving her jittery and off balance.

And then there was Cal. Pouring on enough maple syrup to drown his pancakes rather than flavor them. If she ate even a bite of that, her system would go sugar-shock catatonic in a moment.

She'd driven her MINI back into town, not trusting herself to drive Cal's car in her current state. Parking beside the diner let her approach mostly along the covered, wraparound porch. It had also let her see Cal rushing across the street wearing nothing but a t-shirt despite the storm. He'd been in a real hurry, more than could be explained by a cold rain.

For her. He'd been in a hurry for her. At least that's what she'd thought until he'd slammed the door in her face. Well, if he wanted to play that game, so could she.

"Heading to sleep after this," she told Jessica, "just haven't gone to bed yet. Had some ideas for a project at work and wanted to get them up on the server. You know, Jess," she kept her voice as nonchalant as possible while keeping a weather eye on Cal as he started to dig into his tall stack. "The weekend was so crazy that we didn't get a chance to do anything but the wedding. What are you and Greg doing for dinner tonight?"

Cal froze with his fork caught between his teeth.

Jessica and Greg traded shrugs. "*Nada.*"

"Great! The *three* of us should get together for a meal."

Cal choked loudly on his pancakes. So, he had assumed that she'd be spending the night with him without his even asking.

Jessica had looked puzzled at Natalya's emphasis on just the three of them. Then her expression shifted while Cal coughed and gagged. When he gasped as he tried to rinse it all down with a slug of blazing hot coffee, it was one clue too many.

Jessica had always been sharp. At the moment, as she turned to stare at Natalya, too sharp. Without even looking, Jessica poured a glass of water and thunked it on the counter beside Cal's coffee.

Then she smirked. Over the initial shock, she saw right through the tease of Natalya asking Greg and herself to dinner.

"Man doesn't even know how to eat pancakes without hurting himself," Jessica picked up some menus and went to greet the latest arrivals.

Natalya reached over kindly and pounded a side-fist against Cal's back as hard as she could. It was a mistake. Her fist merely bounced off all that solid muscle which only reminded her of how his bare shoulders had felt beneath her hands while he'd been curled against her. Most of her lovers had been urbanites like her: programmers, designers, gym-machine buff at best. Cal was in a whole different league and it had felt surprisingly good—like finally getting to Italy and understanding that's what gelato *really* tasted like.

An awkward silence slipped between them. Greg was only ten feet away, but the grill and the windowed opening gave some feeling of distance. Also, the big overhead fans made it hard for him to overhear them. He checked on them occasionally, but it was just a chef watching out for his restaurant. He'd missed what was going on. Jessica would fill him in soon enough.

"Hey, Gnat," Cal was decent enough to be the one to break the silence.

" 'Hey, Gnat?' That's all you have to offer after…" Jessica came back to the window with another order and Natalya cut herself off.

Cal waited too, until it was obvious that Jessica was lingering.

"Nothing happened, Jess!" Natalya snapped at her best friend but was too confused to care much. "We danced and we slept together, as in sleep. That's it."

"Which totally doesn't explain why you're awake at six in the morning and are being so flustered." And she walked away not even waiting long enough to leave a smug smile along with Natalya's omelette.

"Crap!"

"Sorry, Gnat." And Cal did sound sorry.

"Yeah, Cal," she patted his big arm and wished she didn't have some need to keep patting him. He was cold to the touch and wet, and not in a happy, healthy dog's nose way. "Me too."

"I can't even stay long. I left Dad making bagels on his day off. Guess he just woke up full of energy today."

"Or never went to sleep," Natalya mumbled to herself.

"What was that?"

"Nothing."

Cal worked through a whole section of his tall stack, a daunting task with how big the Puffin Diner served their pancakes, before speaking again. "I was thinking maybe you and I could have dinner."

"Pizza and a quick tumble?"

"Wouldn't find me complaining."

"I was being sarcastic."

"Yeah, your tone kinda said that."

Natalya took a bite of her omelette.

"How about a burger and brew at the Plover?" Cal offered as a compromise. He was many things, but stupid wasn't one of them.

Once he'd calmed down, he too had understood the tease of her pretending to ask Greg and Jessica to dinner. This time his tone was kind.

"My treat. I feel bad about last night. Tried to stay awake. Heard the shower go on, but never heard it turn off. My schedule's a little weird, baker's hours and all. I usually have dinner at five and I'm asleep by nine, not dancing up to midnight. But we could eat anytime you'd like. What time do you eat in the city?" He was rambling a bit. Which meant he was nervous. Nervous about her reaction. At some level he actually cared about her as well as the sex.

It was decent of him. That was another of the things Cal was. He might tease her by letting a door slam in her face, but he hadn't pushed about not having a quickie though she'd been lying against him barely clothed in his bed.

And he'd loaned her his beloved Corvette.

"Portland isn't Paris."

"Which means what to a boy from Eagle Cove?"

"It means I don't eat dinner at ten at night."

"That's a relief."

"More like a nuked burrito at one in the morning."

He groaned, just as she'd planned.

"But five sounds great."

Cal smiled down at her, his face lighting up for the first time as it had at the wedding. "Maybe a tumble afterward?" Pure tease.

"Don't count on it, Bagel Boy."

He tried a pout and she brushed a hand along his cheek for being so cute. Unlike his shoulder, it was dry, warm, and soft with just a hint that he hadn't shaved this morning. He might be six-four of powerful man, but he *was* cute. Maybe he wasn't totally foolish in his hopes of getting her into bed tonight.

"Ha!" It just burst out of her.

"What?"

She shook her head and focused on her omelette.

"What?" He said it in a soft, warm voice as if trying to coax her out of her clothes here and now.

Well, he'd already done that once. Besides, she'd originally planned to drive back to the city this afternoon before it got dark. Yet she'd just answered her own question about Cal when she'd agreed to go to dinner with him without a second thought. It meant that she'd be driving back to Portland tomorrow morning before work.

If he used that low, sexy tone on her tonight after dinner, it just might do what he intended. She'd give him fifty-fifty odds at the moment that she wouldn't be leaving from her mom's B&B in the morning.

Chapter 4

Cal went up to the front to close the Blackbird Bakery's curtains. The day had continued wet with a steady Pineapple Express storm slamming in from the general southwest direction of Hawaii. It wasn't a particularly big storm, and while it wasn't raining at the moment, the air was almost as wet as the streets. The cinnamon rolls had been slow to rise in the high humidity and the traffic in the store had been low. Still, he'd estimated fairly well and the day-old rack wouldn't be too full tomorrow.

One of the changes he'd made over the last decade and a half was how much of the bakery business was over the counter. His dad had developed recipes and built up the bakery, but Cal was building a business. He'd made deals to provide toast bread to the Puffin Diner, dessert tarts to the Brass Plover Inn, and even cookies to the snack counter at The Flicker movie house. Blackbird Bakery bread was featured next door in Jane's Warbler Market and he'd had inquiries from Coos Bay and Yachats, but he wasn't interested in doing wide area deliveries. Their orders would have to be big enough to hire a driver, and they weren't.

Sunset had only been ten minutes ago, but it had been behind dark, thick clouds that were promising more rain. The sky was already night-black. The Flicker's marquee was the main light in town, making the eight-foot tall chainsaw-art flicker woodpecker clinging to the sign's side appear to glow in the dark. The Bobbin' Red Robin Tavern, being a land bird, was on the same side of the street as his Blackbird Bakery and The Flicker. Except for the Brass Plover Inn, the other side of the street went suddenly dark even as he watched. Merganser Weavings and Tours and Sandpiper Hearth and Home Supply just closed shop for the day.

There was some debate, on particularly slow nights over a beer at the Plover, whether Bird Beak Taffy belonged with the seabird side of the street or over with the land birds. To add fuel to the fire, Celeste recently—well, while Cal was still in high school so recent enough—had painted a great blue heron on her sign, chewing away on a piece of bright orange taffy. At least most everyone agreed it was a great blue which was a land bird, placing her on the wrong side of the street. But as Celeste's art was abstract at best (really just kinda funky), there was a small but verbal contingent that thought it was a black-necked stilt.

Celeste wasn't saying which she'd intended, which offered everyone at least one point of consensus: they all agreed that Celeste had always been a troublemaker. If only because she made the very best taffy on the coast much to everyone's, except the dentist's, remorse.

Cal closed the curtains to block out the darkness.

He hadn't a clue about what had inspired him at the last minute this morning to ask Natalya to meet him at the closed bakery at five rather than at the Brass Plover Inn, but was glad of it now. Maybe enough of his brain cells had finally been firing to do something right around her for a change.

He had one of the tables set with actual silverware and wineglasses. Unable to scrounge up anything better, they'd be stuck with paper napkins. The place was still warm from the heat of the ovens that had been turned off at noon—except for the small one set to warm with a tray of the Plover's lasagna in it.

Cal wanted to get some private time with Natalya. Going to the Plover felt too public. Everyone would know they'd gone out to dinner together, an event that hadn't happened since group pizza outings in high school. And they'd conjecture many things if he and Natalya crossed the street back to his apartment together afterwards.

He wouldn't mind. Hell, a man who got to lay beside a woman as fine as Natalya definitely had bragging rights.

But he wanted to give Natalya some option about how public she was going to be.

Though it wasn't like they were doing anything. Two old friends having dinner, that's all. Of course after the way they'd been dancing together last night, the whole town would be making assumptions about—

Cal grabbed the door frame ready to pound his head against it to make his whirling thoughts stop when he spotted automobile lights through the door's window. Natalya's MINI cooper slid to a stop at the curb right in front of the darkened bakery's door.

No mistaking who climbed out of that car. Not with those graceful dancer movements and the stylish raincoat. They way she looked as she hurried around the car was—

"What the hell?"

She ducked across the street and headed toward the Brass Plover.

Cal yanked at the door.

And cursed as the deadbolt stopped him.

He undid the bolt and yanked again.

Too hard, the doorknob slipped out of his clumsy grasp and slammed against a table he kept meaning to move. It had one of those wire tourist brochure holders that was always getting knocked askew. This time he bashed it hard enough that it spilled to the floor and a hundred glossy, one-third page cardboard flyers sheeted across the floor mixing Ralph's

Eaglet Fishing Tours with the Newport Aquarium and Peggy's Albatross Air Tours with the Sea Lion Caves.

The wind gusted in and began stirring them about.

He grabbed the door handle, but before he could shout out to Natalya a blast of rain slapped him in face. When he could see again, she was gone.

"Shit!" He yanked the door closed behind him as he raced out into the night and across the street.

# # #

Natalya had stumbled to a halt when she entered the Plover. The warmth was almost a wall to hold you up after ducking through the cold rain.

May Conklin had decorated the Brass Plover like a British pub. Comfortably battered booths lined the walls. Tables small enough to be easily dragged into larger groupings were scattered over most of the floor in a pleasantly disorderly jumble. The walls were covered with pictures of the Queen, the royal family, British Navy ships, beautiful coastlines, and a whole section dedicated to the princes—especially William: in his military helicopter, with Kate, and with the kids. Princess Di was also prominent, though Charles was rightly nearly invisible and Camilla nonexistent.

The lights were set low enough to give the feel of oil lamps without quite tipping from cozy into dingy. The dark wood bar—supposedly shaped from the decking of a three-masted lumber schooner that had wrecked on Orca Head over a century ago—ranged down one wall. She had several imported beers, but most of them were Becky's.

The pub's wall of warmth and coziness after the chilling winter storm was built on a foundation of the rich smells of comfort food. May's kitchen served up a mixture of English fare including: fish and chips, shepherd's pie, and bangers and mashies as well as burgers. The burger meat varied by what was fresh: grass-fed beef, venison, elk, and occasionally buffalo. She also, in honor of her great-great-grandfather who had wagon-trained out of Buffalo, New York, and down the Oregon Trail, served lethally spicy chicken wings.

A dozen or so people had come out for a beer or dinner. Locals were used to the heavy rains of the coast, so it would take more than this storm to stop them coming out. Instead they'd used the foul weather as an excuse to gather at the Plover.

Natalya spotted Greg and Jessica, but there was no sign of Cal.

She checked again, but her eyes were dark-adapted from the overcast evening. She hadn't missed him, not that it was possible to miss a man built on his scale.

Greg's wave drew her to their table. "Hey there, Natalya. Dinner was a great idea. Jessica was so glad of a chance to catch up with you." He said it as if her morning ploy to tease Cal by going to dinner with Greg and Jessica had been serious.

But Jessica knew—

And that's when Natalya saw that Jessica absolutely *did* know that Natalya had been teasing and this was supposed to be a date with Cal. Worse, Jessica hadn't informed Greg because he'd be too decent to butt in.

Not Jessica.

Resigned, Natalya shed her coat and slipped in to sit across from her.

"Bitch," she mouthed.

Jessica smiled happily as if it was a compliment.

Greg missed it all. He was busy waving toward the door, "Hey Cal! Well, this will be a great meal."

Natalya waited until Cal stood at the end of the table before turning to look up at him. Then she laughed in his face.

"What?" It came out as deep, irritated-as-hell man-growl.

"You're all wet again." His light hair was darkly wet and plastered to his head. The black t-shirt clung to every curve of muscle. It had a big heart with white lettering in the center of it made up of baking words: vanilla, honey, flour, cinnamon, and more. Her fingers itched to take it off him, squeeze it out, and wrap him in a warm towel. He looked so sad and bedraggled.

"You *weren't* kidding." Cal glanced at Greg and Jessica then looked back at her. She could see that he was about to turn and go, thinking she'd actually planned this.

"Yes, I was. Jessica is just a buttinski."

Cal glared down at Greg who finally put two and two together and realized that it equaled two people too many on a date. "Shit, man. Sorry. I didn't get it. Come on, Jessica."

He started to rise, but Cal just pushed him gently back into his seat. He glared down at Natalya until she became aware of the hardness of the seat and that her hair lay wet against her back.

"What?"

"Then why did you come here instead of to the bakery?"

"The bakery?" And then it clicked. As he'd walked her back to her car, Cal had asked her to meet him at the bakery. Had some plan…that she'd screwed up by coming here instead.

"Oh god. I'm sorry, Cal," she reached out a hand and rested it on his damp forearm. "If you're going to date me, there's something you have to learn. You can't be telling me something at six in the morning and expect that there's any chance in the world I'll remember it."

"Ah ha!" Jessica crowed. "You two are dating!"

"Not yet," Natalya looked up at Cal carefully. "Unless you want to sit down and share dinner with me."

"Truth, Gnat?"

"Absolute truth, Cal," Jessica answered for her. "That's why I was so shocked to see her at the diner this morning. At that hour she usually can't remember her own name."

"Truth, Cal," Natalya answered for herself. "Never anything but."

"She also can't lie to save her life," Jessica pointed at the open chair in a peremptory gesture. "That's why she never tries."

Cal sat. Close enough for Natalya to feel his cool dampness though they weren't quite touching.

"Why do you think she had to perfect that ever-so-innocent smile?" Jessica was happily carrying the conversation which was a relief at the moment.

Natalya wondered just what plan of Cal's she'd messed up. Well, she had a few plans of her own for later and was hoping that she hadn't messed those up herself.

"If she spoke," Jessica continued, "you'd know she was fibbing."

"That so?" Cal seemed to have forgiven her brainlessness, which was awfully decent of him. She definitely owed him.

"Sure," Natalya admitted. "Learned that the hard way when I tried to pull one over on Mrs. Winslow back in second grade. I then made the mistake of trying to talk my way out of it."

"Didn't go so well, huh?"

"Don't you remember the three weeks she spent in the corner wearing a dunce's hat?" Jessica was having too much of a good time at her expense, but Natalya couldn't think of what to do about it. Besides, it had only been for three days.

"Old lady Winslow had it in for me," Cal explained.

"Me too," Greg put in. He'd been three years behind the rest of them, but Marjorie Winslow was still a fixture in the Eagle Cove school system. "She was—"

"Don't you say a word against her," Jessica warned her husband. "She's wonderful."

"Teacher's pet," Natalya got her back a little.

Jessica stuck out her tongue.

"Only thing I remember about you in second grade, Gnat, was you were always borrowing my notes, but when you gave them back they were in mirror writing." Cal laughed at the memory. It was a good laugh and Natalya liked that he used it more and more as they enjoyed their meal together.

# # #

Cal led Natalya back to the bakery at a dead run. She'd offered to hold her coat up as an umbrella for both of them, but he knew the rising wind would snatch it aside and soak them both for spite.

They crashed into the door together—which was odd because he'd grabbed the latch before they hit.

He tried it again as Natalya laughed about the mad race through the rain. But he knew it wouldn't do any good; the deadbolt had snapped into place as he'd slammed the door behind him in his rush to intercept Natalya before she entered the Plover.

"C'mon, Cal. It's cold out here."

"Quit griping, Gnat. At least you have a coat."

"At least one of us has some sense of self-preservation. What's the holdup?"

"My keys."

"What about them?"

"They're on the hook beside my jacket in the back."

"In the back of what?"

Cal looked down at her and wished he was somehow smarter around her. But he wasn't. Natalya brought out the stupid in him.

"In the back of what?" She repeated her question.

"Of the bakery."

She looked from his face, down to his hand still on the door, then back up to his face. For a long moment he couldn't read her expression, then she laid her forehead against his chest and burst into laughter.

Taking a risk, he slipped a hand around her back. Even through the cold, damp raincoat she felt so amazing.

"Running a hell of a seduction here, Mason."

"Yeah, a screwed up one. Of course it was all on track until you went to the Plover by accident."

"And you locked your keys inside. Don't you have a spare hidden somewhere?"

"Sure," Cal could picture it easily even though he'd never used it. He didn't lose or forget things, except around Natalya. "It's in my Vette."

"Which I left at the B&B." Her laugh climbed until it was almost enough to warm him despite wearing a wet t-shirt in a forty-degree windy January night.

He rested his cheek on top of her wet hair, but he couldn't suppress the first shiver.

"C'mon," Natalya pulled back then tugged on his hand, leading him toward her MINI Cooper at the curb.

Cal glared down at the car that barely reached his sternum. Natalya slipped into the car with a, "Try it, you'll like it."

He groaned and bent down to open the door just as Natalya leaned over to slide the seat all of the way back. Cal folded himself up like a pretzel and eased down into the tiny car.

"Sit up, Mason."

Cautiously he raised his head. When it didn't hit, he looked up and saw he had at least an inch to spare. Easing out his legs, only his toes hit the firewall.

"Small car for big people. I'm five-ten, Cal. I like having some space to move around in."

"I'll be damned."

"That's a given," Natalya cranked the engine as he pulled the door shut.

"Heat would be good," he fought down another shiver without much success then buckled in. He might be able to fit in the tiny car, but maneuvering around for seatbelts had him bumping and jostling against Natalya. He could get to really like this.

"Thought you'd be plenty warm from being damned. Besides she's cold, too. Give her a moment. We don't live in Minnesota so I didn't spring for the heated seats."

"Cheapskate," at the moment he'd really appreciate it if they were. "Besides, 'I'll be damned' is future tense."

She eased back from the curb as he cupped his hands over the heater vent. Even the marginally warm air was an improvement.

"Ready?"

"For what?"

She goosed the engine and dropped into first. The car actually chirped its tires despite the wet pavement. She fishtailed once, but handled it expertly and in moments was bolting up the long empty stretch of Beach Way.

Cal hung on as she did a four-wheel slide turn onto LBB Lane and hit the narrow, winding lane like a motocross course.

"Shit, woman!" For half a second he thought she'd miss the last turn south, and instead they'd launch right off the high bank down to the sandy beach and out into the pounding ocean. Third to second, handbrake turn, hard on the gas, back to third, then fourth. They flew off a rise, leapt over potholes, and slalomed through curves.

Somewhere along the way she passed Greg and Jessica despite their significant head start back. The two grand Victorians of the town stood side by side at the very end of LBB Lane: the Lamont B&B and the only slightly less impressive Slater residence just one driveway earlier. She passed them so fast that Cal barely had a glimpse of Greg's alarmed expression.

They covered the two miles to her mom's B&B before the heater had a chance to warm up, and definitely before he caught his breath.

A hundred yards out, she backed off the gas, dropping into a quiet coast, and bled speed until she was parked close beside his Vette. The porch light was blurred by the rain.

"Did you do that to my poor little car?"

"Absolutely! Though I found it kinda sloppy in the turns." And Cal could hear it. "Kinda" was one of his words, not one of hers.

"Jess was right."

"That's news," Natalya turned off the car. "About what?"

"You can't lie for crap."

Natalya sighed, then leaned forward as if to pound her head on the steering wheel. "Frankly, your car scared the daylights out of me and I don't think I made it out of first gear. I knew if I put a single scratch on it, you'd kill me."

"You always were a smart woman, Gnat."

"What?"

He repeated himself more loudly, as the gods had yanked open the heavenly sluice gates and the rain pounded down against the car in solid sheets. The porch light was visible now as little more than a bright spot in the mass of water dumping out of the sky.

They sat quietly for a long moment listening to the pounding rain before she spoke again, nearly shouting, "Well?"

"Well what?"

"Are you going to get the spare key? I'll follow you back to your place if you still want me to." She held out his Corvette's key.

He took it but made no move to get out of the car. The cloudburst continued to pound on the roof.

"Well?"

He leaned forward to look out the front windshield and up. "Maybe we should just stay in the car and neck until this cloudburst moves inland."

Natalya poked a finger against his chest. "Ew! You're still cold and wet."

"Sure are picky, Gnat."

He looked up again at the grand Victorian B&B. "This place here looks pretty warm and cozy. Think they have any beds?"

"I think there's an open room if you want to sleep here. Single or double occupancy?"

"Double." He tried to make light of her joke, but it came out rough and needy.

"Just can't wait, huh?"

He turned to look at her, shadows and shapes as she too leaned forward and looked upward, the curve of her neck making his fingers itch to touch. "To hold you, Gnat. No! I can't wait."

"Last one loses."

"Huh? Last one of what loses wha—" But he was talking to himself. She was out the door and racing across the wet lawn. Cal shoved open the door and almost strangled himself before he remembered the seatbelt.

When he caught up to her in the kitchen, she wasn't waiting for him. He'd expected her to be facing him and had been planning on scooping her up, over his shoulder, and dragging her upstairs.

Instead she was over at the basement door and looking down. It was open, the light was on, and there was a string of loud, heartfelt, female curses sounding up the stairs.

# # #

"Mom? Everything okay?" The exhilaration of racing Cal into the B&B, the anticipation of having him in her bed, faded away abruptly.

"No!"

Natalya made it halfway down the stairs before she saw why. Six inches of water was flowing through the basement. It was an old problem that she'd forgotten about over the years. A French drain around the outside had diverted some of the water and a sump pump usually took care of the rest, but this whole side of Orca Head and the surrounding forest wanted to drain right through the B&B's basement tonight.

Her mother was standing in the middle of the mess wearing coveralls, waders, yellow dishwashing gloves, and a foul expression. Thankfully, they'd had the problem before so the lowest level of all of the shelving around the room was empty. But if it kept rising, it could be disastrous.

"The sump pump clogged or failed. Or maybe it just drowned. I can't tell."

Natalya wouldn't be of any help. Mechanical things and she didn't get along very well. She was well known at her job for her ability to break computers that worked fine for everyone else.

Cal had come down the stairs behind Natalya and was surveying the scene. Without a word, he gently pushed her to the side and continued down, wading right into the water in his tennis shoes.

The next few hours were a scene fit for a Victorian steampunk disaster.

Natalya had fetched a second pair of her mother's boots, more gloves, and soon the both of them were dipping up buckets of water and dumping them down the laundry sink.

The chill water kept rising until it finally tipped over the tops of her boots as often as not, and it was a race to save the furnace and water heater which weren't on the floor, but weren't much above the water either.

Natalya's arms burned with the workout. Bits of paper and plastic junk floated along the surface and they were soon clogging the sink. She was cold, wet, and on the verge of telling her mom to either call the fire department for one of their pumpers or find some dynamite to blast a hole in the seaward wall to let it all drain out.

All the while she and her mom had been bailing, Cal was squatting half in and half out of the water, often reaching down shoulder deep to work on the pump which sat another foot below the floor in a sump.

Then a hum sounded, a deep, powerful hum. One she could practically feel in her bones.

And Cal was standing there, calf deep in the water, soaking wet, and grinning like a fool as he stared down at a small whirlpool in the water. In moments she could see the surface water flowing toward the pump as it dug in and did its job.

Her mom shrieked with delight and grabbed Cal in a hard hug.

Natalya could only stand and watch.

A man with skills. There was something about a man with skills. A big, handsome man whose head almost brushed the low basement ceiling that just made her knees go weak.

They all stood and watched as the water level dropped until finally, it was just little trickles and puddles on the concrete floor. With a self-satisfied burp, the pump shut down. With a broom, Cal swept the larger puddles toward the sump. It cycled on automatically for a few seconds and then shut down again finding the job too easy.

It was when they were climbing the stairs that Natalya understood quite how weak her knees were, and it wasn't just Cal's macho influence.

# # #

Cal focused on putting one foot in front of the other. The water had been damned cold. And he had to keep ducking down into it. The pump's float switch had broken and he'd pretty much had to rebuild it under water.

Up the basement stairs. It was a vast relief when the door closed and they were done with the basement. He passed up Gina's offer of hot cocoa or tea in favor of a shower. Besides, Natalya was staggering, so he slipped a hand around her waist as she led them up the stairs. The two more stories up the stairways of the B&B took almost all she had left, but he didn't think he was up to carrying her right at the moment. And if she hadn't liked that he'd been wet before, he was thoroughly soaked now.

Just like him before, Natalya didn't bother to turn on lights. However, the flight to his apartment was one clean shot. These stairs were bent on pitching him overboard with twists and turns in odd places.

He knew the ground floor well, of course. Gina Lamont's parties were notorious and he and Dad had tried to never miss a one. Though the last one had been a while. It had been Greg's wedding to Jessica three months ago, an event that had packed the house, the porch, and spilled out over the lawn. It was also when Harry—back visiting for his little brother's wedding—had fallen for Becky Billings.

As if he'd needed proof that weddings were dangerous.

"Do you live in this place or one top of it?"

"Third floor," Natalya led him up the last few steps. "Mom always said that just because we lived in a B&B didn't mean we were supposed to have the crappiest rooms. She's always had the suite on the northwest corner of the second floor, three rooms which has one of the balconies facing out toward the ocean. I've got third floor, southwest corner, view of the beach and Orca Head lighthouse. Mom rents it out last of all, so I usually get to stay in my old room during the off season."

The third floor hallway wasn't really wide enough for the two of them but he wasn't willing to let her go. Didn't know if he dared—half afraid that she'd evaporate into thin air and more than half afraid he'd slide bonelessly to the carpet if she did that.

He'd never been up here on the top floor. In all the years he'd known her, he'd never been up to her room. In the darkness, their path indicated by a few small nightlights that illuminated no more than the floral green runner and the dark oak floors, he felt as if he'd wandered into *The Adams Family* and Uncle Fester would come stumbling out the next door along the hall at any moment.

He could just make out the sign on the door to the last room at the end of the hall: The Victorian Room.

"Victorian, huh? Curtained four-poster and chintz curtains?"

"Not quite," Natalya turned on the lights and guided him over the threshold.

The bed wasn't a four-poster, but it did have an ornate, padded headboard, which would have given him a few ideas under different conditions. And it did feel "classic" with dark wood and a broad oriental rug on the hardwood. But then he focused on the rest of the décor.

Rachel McAdams inspected him from a Sherlock Holmes movie poster in which she played the sexy yet dangerous Irene Adler. Selma Hayek wore a stunning Victorian dress in the terrible *Wild Wild West* remake.

"I started when I was about ten, collecting Victorian and steampunk images."

Winona Ryder as Jo Marsh was hunched over her writer's desk, feathered quill in hand, scribing out her own story in *Little Women.* He'd gotten snookered into watching it while on a Kirsten Dunst movie binge. Nicole Kidman in *Moulin Rouge,* not the sad but fallen woman, instead the grand beauty caught mid-laugh.

There were also drawings of steampunked women. Their garb half Victorian and half mechanical. Their powerful expressions undeniable.

But that wasn't what captured his attention as he forgot for a moment quite how cold he was. Mixed in among the posters were sketches and paintings. Some were pen and ink, others were fine creations on canvas. And he knew the hand of all of them.

Natalya.

She disappeared into the bathroom as a shiver shook him. He crossed his arms over his chest and kept inspecting the walls. He could see the evolution of the artist. Early drawings of elves and princesses had been preserved. They'd given away to occasional monsters, he recognized a far more polished version of the one she'd drawn of him that day in the woods—not recognizable as either himself or her mother, but now artful. Steampunk and Victorian women abounded. Many had a breathtaking beauty. Not that every one of the images was pretty, but these were strong women whose very expressions were forces of nature.

Natalya reemerged from the bath long enough to toss a towel over his head. She was now wrapped in a towel. Thinking back, he had heard her taking a lightning fast shower.

By the time he pulled off the towel, she was gone again. He scrubbed the towel at his hair and face for a moment, then began peeling off his soaking wet clothes.

His attention drifted back to the most recent paintings. They were different. Still the same artist, but the content had shifted again. The Oregon Coast replaced the dust and grime of the Victorian era. They were portraits. Sometimes from the back, but they were again of women. Each one…belonged. He didn't have a better word for it. Having seen them in their setting, they couldn't be anywhere else.

"Hey, Gnat. These are really—" He turned his attention to Natalya and completely forgot what he'd been about to say.

Wearing a long t-shirt that was far skimpier on her than his had been, she was sliding into the bed.

"Damn you're a vision."

If she heard him, she didn't acknowledge it, instead pulling the covers over her head and huddling beneath them.

Cal hurried through a scalding hot shower. Even his underwear was wet and he didn't want to wear it anyway. Naked, he slid under the covers and reached out to pull Natalya against him.

Except she wasn't responding. She wasn't just asleep, she was out cold. The wedding, only a few hours sleep last night, and two hours of mucking about in freezing water.

"Crap!"

He curled up behind her and buried his nose in her hair—which was cold and damp and had him jerking back.

Giving up, he collapsed onto the pillow and was out.

Chapter 5

A low cello started out somewhere in a dream about tiny cars with giant blackbird wings swooping over a field of baked goods—diving like raptors to clutch giant blueberries.

A pair of violins joined the flight and Cal came fully awake in time for a viola to join in and for the MINI Cooper to steal the last berry before his Vette could get there, leaving nothing but a stray sunflower seed behind.

The cars were gone, but the music continued—upbeat, energetic.

Cal didn't know this one. Didn't recall putting it on his playlist.

He reached over to see what it was and bumped his arm on someone curled up close beside him. Some—

Natalya! Again they had slept together and not crap else. This was really starting to suck.

"Mrumph!" was all she gave him in response.

Damn it! He didn't want stolen seconds with her. He wanted time to enjoy himself and make sure that she did the same.

All he'd had a chance to do yesterday morning was hold onto her for a few minutes. Last night he hadn't stayed awake long enough to even do that. It looked as if today he was in for another serving of the same. He'd take what he could get.

Her back was pressed against his arm, so he curled up behind her and wrapped an arm around her waist. He'd always been partial to long and slender, and Natalya was definitely that.

A drummer joined the quartet and the energy climbed again. And not just the music's.

She woke enough to push back against him. She rested her head on his extended arm, which let him nuzzle his face into her hair, and then she shifted the rest of her body up against him. When his rousing interest pressed up against her backside she made another noise; one that he'd judge as contented rather than bothered.

He ran a hand down over her thigh and, after only the briefest consideration, came back up under her t-shirt rather than over it. Most women on a cold night were like a good sports balm after a hard soccer game. Natalya Lamont, warm and sleepy beneath the covers, was in a whole other league. Of its own will, his hand stopped spread across her flat belly, long before it reached his actual target. He became mesmerized by the feel of her breathing.

He buried his face deeper in her hair—soft and dry now— inhaled the ocean clean scent of her, and pulled her even harder against him.

This time it earned him a definite happy sound.

She lay on his bicep, so he took advantage of the moment and bent his elbow around to gather himself a palmful of breast through the t-shirt fabric with his left hand while his right remained on her stomach.

A sleepy sigh and she slipped a hand over his. Rather than moving it, she just rubbed her palm lazily up and down his arm.

"You're killing me, Gnat. You're just killing me."

"Good," it was a soft, quiet whisper, but she sounded very pleased with herself.

Without enough time, he again wasn't going to get more than a quick feel. Which sucked, because it was a really amazing feel. To back off from his need to just take her now and the consequences be damned, he asked her about the music.

"All-girl string quartets," her voice was part sleepy mumble and part breathy seductress—at least that was his body's response. "Mostly Bond, some Escala, and a few others. And why are you clamped onto my breast but we're suddenly talking about music?"

"The alarm. I have to go to work."

"Sure," and she paused maddeningly. "In an hour. I set the alarm an hour early, and I want you to remember quite how big a sacrifice that was for me. But since you're so interested, let me tell you about the four women of Bond. Australian and British. Two tall, two not so much."

An hour! "I had no idea you were brilliant in addition to being beautiful." He could really get to appreciate this woman.

"Two blond, two brunette," she continued as if she hadn't heard him.

Cal could do plenty with an hour. Not near what he wanted, but it would be a good start.

"Their videos—"

"Please tell me you have some protection here. I don't want to waste the time dragging you back to my place."

"Of course I do, Mason. I'm not some idiot who locks himself out of his own house. Now, Escala's music videos are good, but Bond's are awesome, very sensual yet still all about the music itself. Amazing marketing. You should watch them play."

Cal held onto her tightly and tried to make sense of what in the world she was talking about.

"Here, let me grab my tablet, I can show you some," and she moved to get out of a bed.

He almost let her go. The woman was an absolute primal force. *Idiot! She's just messing with you!*

Two could play that game. So he let her get half away, then three quarters. He could feel her hesitating as he continued to call her bluff. Then he felt the shift from teasing to ticked. That was his cue. He lunged out, grabbed, and scooped her back against him so hard that it knocked some of the breath out of her. He took advantage of the moment to flip her over so that they were face to face.

"Maybe another time," she managed on a gasp. "Though I bet you'd like the little Asian cellist. She's—"

The only way he could think to silence her was to kiss her, hard. As she opened to him, she might have mumbled, "About time."

After that her focus was absolute.

Against a background of soaring, exotic music, they explored, played, and gasped in shared delight. When he finally took her, or perhaps she took him for he was the one flat on his back, the world went quiet.

Somewhere in the far distance the music continued, but the world of sensation overwhelmed and he was only aware of the searing heat where she wrapped around him and the lovely light weight of her as he supported her with his palms cradling her breasts.

Her hair teased over his chest as she hung her head and gave herself to the dynamic building between them. She didn't cry out or moan.

Instead, she whispered as the release wracked through her body, "So good. Oh, so good. So…good."

As her words dissolved into odd mumbles and finally a shuddering silence, it made him feel as if maybe he really was a good lover. To have the power to drive Natalya Lamont beyond the ability of speech must mean he was doing something right. So very right.

And the more he felt that, the more true it became. She drove her hips down hard against him again and again until all he could do was arch up into her and lose himself as well.

When Cal finally found his way back to reality, Natalya lay upon his chest, her knees alongside his hips, and his hands scooped around the nicest butt he'd ever held.

"Damn, Mason."

"Damn yourself, Gnat. That was…unreal." Best he had. And it was true. He and sex certainly weren't strangers. He'd had more than his fair share of the locals over the years and was thankful for every one. There'd been any number of cute tourists who were willing to offer their buns for a little quick kneading. He'd thought he knew all that it could deliver. Not really. Not even close. Natalya had just completely redefined the reality of sex.

"We definitely have to do this again," she planted a kiss on his chin.

"Uh-huh," he couldn't agree more. "How much time do we have?"

She turned her face into his shoulder and giggled. He'd never heard her giggle. Natalya Lamont smiled quietly when one of her pranks worked, which was pretty much every time. She laughed quietly at a good joke. But now she lay on his chest and giggled. Cute on top of gorgeous.

"Okay. Not enough time."

"Hell, I'm ready to do that all over again, Mason. You could almost convince me that waking up in the middle of the night is totally worth it. But you're a guy. What are we going to do about *that?*"

Well, parts of his body weren't up for a rematch, but he wasn't ready to let go of her yet. He lifted her off him, and set her down on the bed still face down. Then he sat up and began running his hands over her. Training as a baker had given him a real awareness of texture and pressure through his fingers. He'd been told by more than a few women that he should have been a masseur.

So, he turned his attention to learning about Natalya's body. Unlike others he'd been with, he felt no hesitation in what he did and didn't touch. You could stroke a woman's ass all you wanted during sex, but not during a massage, even if you'd just had sex. Somehow those inhibitions didn't apply here.

# # #

Cal's strength as he simply lifted Natalya aside knocked her speechless. She wasn't overweight, but she wasn't a size zero model either, yet he'd picked her up as easily as a tray of bread. She wasn't ready to be done with him and was about to protest until Cal began running his hands over her as if he were a bow to her fiddle—which was still playing in the background. It was a long playlist; she'd never been one to wake up quickly.

Then Cal drove his fingers deep into her hair and began massaging her scalp. Absolute heaven. She buried her face in the pillow and gave herself up to the experience.

She could feel her whole body tingling in anticipation when it became clear he wasn't going to stop there.

Her shoulder muscles gave way beneath the onslaught of his baker's hands. During sex she'd been busy appreciating so much that his hands had blurred into the background, except to notice that they were gentle despite their immense strength. Now they probed and eased tight muscles. He slipped his hands between the sheets and the front of her shoulders to loosen pectoral muscles already gone liquid. When he used the opportunity to cop an extra feel of her breast, she rocked to the side to make it easier for him.

Her lower back, often sore from too many hours in the computer chair, eased and loosened. When he dug strong fingers into her behind she considered protesting, but the steady assurance of his hands working her muscles brushed even that consideration aside. Also, the pressure against the mattress was such a very nice reminder of how it had felt to take all of Cal into her.

It had been a submission on a grand scale, but also an empowerment. To let a man invade past the boundary of her skin had always felt like a slightly unjust twist of evolution.

Yet, to have Cal inside her, to feel such a deep connection and to hear his breath catch with her every movement, had also made her feel so strong. The galvanic clenching of his body at the moment before his release—wound tighter than a coiled spring powerful enough to run the world—had created a shocking contrast to the moment he let go and poured all of that energy into her. For a brief moment, riding atop the wave of his need, she had been the ruler of the world.

Cal had—

Oh god.

Almost without her awareness he'd slipped a hand between her legs and slid it between her and the sheets.

Too late, unable to stop herself, she rubbed and thrashed against his kneading palm until, unanticipated, another release shot through her. Not nearly the scale of having him buried to his hips inside her, but absolutely breathtaking for being so soon after the first experience.

As she rode it out, or rather as it rode through her again and again, Cal slowly lay back down beside her, leaving gentle kisses and nuzzles as he went.

She clamped her legs together so that he couldn't pull that hand away. Not yet, please not yet. That it forced him to lie awkwardly against her side wasn't her concern. Just the incredible sensation of being held so intimately, so strongly, yet so gently—that's all that mattered.

He nuzzled his nose against her where the side of her breast met the sheets.

She really hadn't been kidding, and if she ever recovered her breath and her mind, she'd have to tell Cal.

They definitely had to do this again.

Chapter 6

C*al left her with* a kiss so sweet that it almost lulled her back to sleep, and a slap on her bare ass that had completely ruined the effect.

Natalya made the bed, because the mussed sheets made her wish Cal was still in them. She then plunged into the shower so that she wouldn't be one of those pitiful women listening for the sound of his car driving away at four in the morning. She did come out of the bath wrapped in a towel, just in case he'd returned, forgetting who knew what this time.

Instead of Cal, her mother was sitting on the quilt, leaning back against the padded headboard, and sipping from a mug of coffee—her favorite, declaring, "It's True! Redheads *ARE* Hotter!" in little flaming letters.

"Um, hi."

"Um, yourself. Saw Cal on the way out, gave him some coffee. Did you have fun?"

Natalya decided to ignore the palm print she could still feel on her behind, and simply nodded her head.

Natalya toed the pile of her clothes, all wet.

"I brought you fresh ones," her mom pointed toward the suitcase by the door. She'd put it in the car last night, assuming that she'd be leaving from Cal's this morning. "Cal said you might need them. I caught him headed back up the stairs with them."

"Uh, thanks." She supposed that their intentions had been made clear enough last night that any embarrassment this morning would be wasted effort.

"Coffee for you, too," her mother rightly assessed Natalya as being momentarily overwhelmed and pointed to a steaming mug on the nightstand. It declared, "Brunettes Are Da BOMB!" complete with an explosion in the background.

"Thanks again. I need that."

Natalya settled on the bed and tucked her legs under the quilt. It was a crazy thing from high school days. She'd gotten into the scraps box and decided to teach herself a dozen quilting patterns from a book. Each block of the quilt was different, each themed with crazily mismatched fabrics: Monkey Wrench, Log Cabin, Bear's Paw, Flying Geese. Friendship Square (pieced in her, Jessica's, and Becky's favorite colors), Mother's Dream (which looked nothing like her mother or a dream, but a much younger Natalya had liked the name…still did).

Her mom rose off the bed just for a moment so that she too could tuck her legs under the quilt. This was familiar; this was family. Just her and Mom together.

Somehow Gina Lamont always knew when Natalya needed a Mom-dose and just showed up.

Natalya's first kiss, not counting Jessica when they tried to practice on one another before trying it out on a boy—which had turned out to be beyond weird and could still set them both giggling. The first crush followed closely by the first heartbreak when she'd been dumped a week later. The first time she'd given herself to a boy. Even when something had gone terribly wrong as an adult living in Portland. Mom would somehow know and… show up. "I had a few city errands to run," which they both knew was a lie. Then they'd sit together and she'd remember that the Lamont women always had each other.

"Do you ever regret it, Mom?"

"What, not marrying Tud? Not for a second."

"Okay, not quite the question I was asking."

"Still, you're twenty-nine now, it's about time I answered it. You were conceived, baked, and born out of wedlock and I don't regret it for a second because you were worth every second of it…well, maybe not the seventeen hours of labor, but otherwise totally worth it. But what were you asking?"

"I'm thirty-two, Mom. And I was asking if you were sorry that you didn't ever bring someone home to keep."

"No daughter of mine will ever be more than twenty-nine. Makes me feel too old." She sipped at her coffee for a bit.

Natalya did the same and felt the smooth warmth slide down into her—two sugars and a splootch of cream just the way she liked it. " 'No daughter of yours?' Any half sisters I should know about?"

"Not a one. Unless you count my twin sister's kids that she had with Tud."

Natalya almost bobbled her cup.

"Just joking. I know Viv slept with him a couple times—a lot of women did and probably a few men. Not your other aunt though, Jessica's mom. My little sister Monica never did have much imagination when it came to men."

Jessica's mother had married Ralph Baxter straight out of high school. Between them they had three divorces and four marriages—all to each other.

"As I said," her mother continued, "Tud had no scruples but was so very pretty. Of course that was before my twin's plane went down in New Guinea and she was eaten by those cannibals."

Natalya knew that Aunt Viv had died in a car crash in Italy when Natalya was two, but her mother was always giving her sister strange and spectacular ways of dying, though the fictitious offspring were new. Perhaps it was her mom's idea of a gift to the dead, keeping her twin's story alive and ever changing. As much as Natalya loved her mom, it was hard to imagine what Eagle Cove had been like with two of her in it. A pair of statuesque redheads with big laughs and a devil-may-care-but-women-didn't-need-to attitude.

Natalya supposed that she never should have asked her question in the first place.

"So, are you that serious about Cal Jr.?" Her mom took advantage of Natalya's silence for her own question.

"What? No! We only had sex once. I'm not enough of an idiot to think that means anything."

"Then where were you two nights ago?"

"Sleeping." Natalya groaned at having to explain it again when she could barely explain it to herself. "Just sleeping."

"But with Cal Jr."

"Yes, with Cal Jr."

"And was it wonderful?"

"He gets up at four a.m. to an alarm playlist filled with early Beach Boys and Andrews Sisters singing about food."

"Probably includes Dean Martin singing, *How D'ya Like Your Eggs in the Morning.*"

"Doris Day, *A Bushel and a Peck.*"

"Harry Chapin, *30,000 Pounds of Bananas.*"

Natalya tried to think of a one-up to that but the giggles caught her again which was okay, she couldn't think of one anyway. "Imagine waking up to that!"

"Stay with him long enough, and maybe you will."

"Eww!" Though it had been awfully nice waking up next to him this morning.

Her mother bumped her shoulder to shoulder, but didn't say another word.

"Okay!" Natalya struggled out from under the quilt and began dragging on dry clothes. "Yes, I'm thinking about seeing him again. But right now I have to get back to Portland for a nine a.m. meeting. Sure he was fun, but I don't see any software companies opening major divisions in Eagle Cove."

"Not this week anyway."

She eyed her mother. Natalya couldn't always read her mom, but this time it was merely a joke. "Besides, I don't want a weekend relationship. I want someone to curl up next to every night." Which surprised the crap out of her now that she'd said it.

"You always did have that in you, Natalya," her mother got up and tugged the quilt back into shape. If a guest needed the room, it would be cleaned and sheets changed then. Probably through the whole stormy winter it would just be Natalya's. "That desire for stability." Natalya didn't like the flash of sadness across her mother's face and circled around the bed to hug her hard.

"You gave me great stability, Mom. Maybe *that's* the problem. I grew up in this house, in this community. I'm thir—twenty-nine and I still have my own room most of the time complete with my old art and the crazed quilt."

Her mom looked down at the quilt. "Yep! Natalya's brain on quilting. Still makes me wonder sometimes what it must be like living inside your head."

"Very cluttered."

"Well, declutter it now. You have a long, dark drive ahead of you. Be extra careful and text me when you're off the road."

"Love you too, Mom." She gathered her things and headed out the door.

The rain had stopped, which was a good thing. Driving over the twists of Maxine Pass in the dark was challenging enough to Natalya's dreamy state without being blinded by the rain as well. The eight-hundred-and-three foot crest was one of the highest that punched through the Coast Range. The rain down below had turned into snow up here.

She considered doubling back down to Highway 101 and chasing north to one of the lower passes, but the only sure way around the snow was way out to Astoria. She didn't have the extra two hours it would require to go so far north before doubling back on Portland. Instead she caught up with a sanding truck and stayed just far enough back to not have her windshield pinged with sand and gravel.

The road through the mountains was usually the fun part of her drive. The MINI Cooper digging in and growling its way around the sharp curves like a grumpy basset hound—low-slung and surprisingly quick. Not today.

Leaving Eagle Cove behind was being much more difficult than usual. And oddly, the hardest part of all hadn't been driving away from the lone light still shining out her mother's bedroom window at the B&B, but rather driving out along Beach Way and seeing the light in the Blackbird Bakery.

She knew stopping in wouldn't be a good thing to do—but for the whole climb up and over the pass and the descent back out of the snow as she reached the Willamette Valley she was wondering how she knew that to be true.

Chapter 7

"Deal 'em!" Cal chewed on a Red Vine. Greg had brought a fat plastic bucket of the damned licorice whips and they'd all been chowing down on them.

The big round table in the center of the closed bakery looked like a bomb had exploded on it. They were playing around the corners of a couple of well-decimated pizza boxes from Carrier Pigeon Pizza, which didn't deliver despite their name, except to Cal. It had been part of the deal he worked out because they used his big mixer when making up fresh batches of dough and he made all of their garlic bread. It wasn't a real burden as they were only two doors apart, sharing a covered porch with the Bobbin' Red Robin Tavern in between.

None of them were heavy drinkers any more, but it was Friday night and each had a beer and an empty or two that no one had bothered to clear off. A roll of paper towels was partially unraveled because no one had wanted to get up for the paper plates Cal had forgotten to grab. They all wore a couple of layers, turtlenecks and flannel shirts or fleece vests.

Rain slicks and empty pizza boxes were piled on the other tables near them.

Harry riffled the cards again. Then set them down to take another bite of his Cowboy Special, which was a whole lot of good, greasy meat.

"Wipe your hand before you—Aw shit!"

Harry offered him a literally cheesy smile and went back to shuffling the cards with slimy fingers.

"Asshole!" Just for that, Cal wasn't going to tell him about the cheese caught in the ridiculous two-week mustache he'd started while on his honeymoon. There were a lot of bets around the table as to who would make him shave it off first, his new wife or his father because "such an affectation would not be appropriate for the bench."

"Take any advantage I can get."

"Not gonna help *me* any." And nothing was tonight. Even though it was a low stakes game, Cal was down at least twenty bucks. Greg was up five, Vincent about ten. His only consolation was that Harry was down even more than he was.

The one sweeping the damned table was Alex.

"Damn it! You used to work for me! And this is how you pay me back?"

Alex raked in the latest pot, putting him up at least forty for the night. "Well, you aren't paying me any more, Becky is. Only way I got left to take money off you."

"You were always a crap baker anyway," he grumbled though they both knew it wasn't true.

He'd been good enough, but his heart wasn't in it. Becky had needed help and he'd sent Alex her way. He'd taken to brewing like a seal to a sunny sandbar.

"Bastard is shacked up with *my* senior prom date," Greg sounded irritated, but probably by the fact that Alex's flush had just beaten his straight.

"Crap, Greg! You're married to Jessica Baxter and you're complaining?" Harry cuffed his brother on the back of the head.

"Not for a second. But," Greg slapped him back, "aren't you supposed to be thinking about *your* new wife?"

Harry sighed happily and started dealing the next hand, "I am, Brother. I really am."

That was when it struck Cal that he was the only single guy left at the table. Greg and Harry were recently married. Vincent had somehow captured the awesome Dawn way back in high school and they had two of the cutest twin girls imaginable—perfect seven-year-old copies of their stunning mother. And Alex had just "shacked up" with Vicki Highland. The main reason Cal had sent him Becky's way was so that Alex and Vicki's work schedules could mesh—Alex was saving for the ring before popping the question even though they were all after him to hurry it up.

But no one wanted a guy working baker's hours.

Not even Natalya Lamont.

Two weeks and not a peep. No e-mail. No phone call. She hadn't come back to town last weekend as he'd been hoping.

Maybe he'd head over to the B&B later, ask Gina for Natalya's phone number as casually as he could. Maybe he'd just take the Vette out for a spin up to Portland and knock on her door, if he knew where she lived.

Cal checked his hole cards: two of clubs, nine of hearts.

He should just fold, lose his fifty-cent ante, and be glad he got off easy.

Being a complete sucker, he threw another quarter in, bad money after good because sure as dough rose, he held a losing hand.

# # #

Natalya stood in the shadows of the Blackbird Bakery's porch and looked in at the game.

It was *such* a guy moment.

It gave her an idea for a painting, not that she'd really had time to do that these last couple years. But maybe this weekend she'd fish out her easel and give it a try because the image was so pure. Not the softness of watercolor. No, this would best be rendered oil…no, acrylics. The dark of the wooden table, the brightness of the lights, and the flashing tiny cards. Contrast the warm mid-tones of laughing faces and easy banter. The green fleece of Harry's vest and Cal's red-and-black flannel shirt as if he were a rough lumberjack rather than a man who shaped puff pastries for a living.

She'd been surprised into stopping when she saw the lights on in the bakery despite it being eight at night.

Fibber. That wasn't what had happened at all.

She sighed. She'd gone to work early (arriving at the office at the obscene hour of seven in the morning) so that she could leave early to beat the weekend traffic south—which hadn't paid off as well as she'd hoped. The three-hour drive had taken almost five as there'd been dumping rain in Portland and ice up in the pass. The coast was a dry and balmy forty-five.

Natalya had driven by slowly, trying to decide on whether or not she really was going to stop and knock on his door. Not as if he'd be expecting her. Showing up with a "Hey, that was some amazing sex, let's have more," was too schoolgirl. Too needy. But she'd slowed anyway.

She'd even braced herself to find another woman's car parked at the bakery. After all, they'd made no promises. But when she spotted four cars and the downstairs alight, curiosity had mixed with caution. She'd parked in front of Carrier Pigeon Pizza and casually walked back to peek in the window.

Harry was hooting with laughter, jostling his brother in his triumph. Vincent and Alex tossed their cards in.

Cal sat with his back squarely to the door. All she could see were his broad shoulders and the back of his head. She remembered how it had felt to wrap her hands about him as they'd danced, how those shoulders felt when she—

Disgusted with herself, Natalya turned and strode back to her car.

You didn't drive five hours for sex.

Then why did she?

It was a question she still hadn't answered when she pulled up to the B&B. The lot was packed.

In January?

That made no sense. Not until she recognized a couple of the vehicles. Mrs. Winslow's, Andrea Martin's, and others. Peggy's car, normally identified by its "Eat. Sleep. Fly." bumper sticker, now boasted "Live. Love. Fly." Is that what marriage did to a person?

Why were they all—

It was knitting night!

Tuesday afternoons and Friday evenings were knitting time in Eagle Cove. It was when the knitters of the town came together. It used to always be here at the B&B, but Tuesdays had moved out to Becky's when she'd torn up her knee and the group had never moved back.

Natalya raced up the porch stairs ready to throw herself into their midst.

This is why you came home. Except she hadn't packed her knitting. For that matter she was still working on the cowl she'd started last summer. She could really use that cowl now.

Again she stopped on the porch and looked in through the parlor windows. Everyone was gathered. Unlike the national disaster area that was the boy's poker game, there was an order here. Glasses of wine and cups of tea. Small plates bearing the remains of her mom's lemon cheesecake with the deep purple of Marionberry syrup sat nearby. Napkins and dessert forks all in place. The raucous laughter of the men that she'd been able to hear through the double-paned glass at the bakery was much softer…even one of her mom's laughs that rang out and set everyone off was milder. It was also gentler—not the laugh of card-game triumph, but friendly, inclusive.

This scene Natalya would paint in watercolors. Again she'd start with the rich browns and golds of the classic Victorian furnishings rather than the well-worn tables and scuffed bakery flooring. The bright colors of the yarn, almost distracting the viewers' eyes, but not quite. The heart of the painting would be in the soft joy of the women.

Perhaps even mount the two side by side.

Or a single work that transitioned, melded, and morphed. Dark wood furniture flowing into a dark bakery table. Delicate desserts colliding with surrealistically garish pizza. Both sides would reveal joy: the rough happiness of men undisturbed by having to behave around women, women quietly glad to be with each other.

Then, wholly unlike the bakery, Tiffany happened to glance through the window and spot Natalya beneath the porch light. She waved.

Natalya waved back.

And in moments she'd been swept inside: receiving hugs, having a dinner plate of lasagna made up, and soon tucked in between Jessica and Becky on the big couch.

This was *exactly* why she'd come home.

Except it wasn't.

Chapter 8

*S*even *a.m.*

Ridiculously early. Especially considering she'd woken up at six the prior morning to get her workday done early so that she could drive down to Eagle Cove.

Yet Natalya was awake and was having a hard time denying it.

Saturday! She scowled at her foggy reflection after she'd showered.

Your day off! Her pillow teased her. *Stop making the bed and crawl back in it.*

Instead, she smoothed the quilt, and worked her way downstairs in a plush robe and her elk slippers (complete with brown fuzzy sides, soft ears, and tiny antlers). She heard voices, but they must be in one of the guest rooms as they stopped the moment Natalya creaked one of the old stairs. The B&B was about half full, but the guests wouldn't be stirring outside their rooms yet.

Her mom was just starting breakfast.

"What in the world are you doing up?"

Natalya kept her head down and drove straight for the coffee pot. "I have absolutely no idea." She poured her cup and prepared it with sugar and cream, then held it up to her nose, close her eyes, and just breathed it in.

She leaned her elbows on the counter, and when she felt she could open her eyes again with a chance of seeing anything, looked out the window at the woods as she cradled her warm mug. It was still dark out there. The towering Douglas firs, that she noted with some chagrin still had the common sense to be asleep, were little more than shadowed impressions.

"It's still night out there."

"That's what happens when you get up before the crack of noon," her mother was slicing strips off a slab of Parker's farm-fresh bacon. Natalya couldn't find the energy to help.

"Okay, I do feel bad about that." She buried nose in the coffee again. She often came down from the city so stressed that the main thing she did when home was sleep.

When home.

But she hadn't lived here in over a decade. Four years at Portland State then straight into the local job market. She had a nice one-bedroom apartment—a third-floor walkup in a century-old bricker right in the heart of the Northwest District. Her street was lined with massive heritage trees—tagged, numbered, and protected by the city for their historic majesty. She even had a territorial view to the south and east from a living room smaller than her bedroom here.

But home was Eagle Cove. How had she missed that?

Deep thoughts for seven in the morning. This morning just kept getting worse and worse.

"Mom?"

"Uh-huh?"

"I—"

"What, honey?"

The sympathy, the understanding without even needing to understand had Natalya setting down her coffee and wrapping her arms around her mom. She buried her face in the fluffy kitchen towel Mom always wore over her shoulder when cooking. Natalya had always wondered if it was a holdover from when she'd been an infant.

The soothing hand stroking down her back was just too much and Natalya started to cry.

"Shh, Baby. Shh," her mother rocked her and cradled Natalya's head. The easy familiarity of the motion definitively answered the question about the fluffy towel.

"I don't even know what's wrong," it came out as a choking twist in her throat that was dangerously close to a sob. Natalya dug deep and tried to reel it back. She knew that for Gina Lamont this was maybe a little too real. As much as she loved to laugh, tears always kind of freaked her mother out. Natalya finally clamped it down but hung on for a while longer simply enjoying the feeling of being held.

"You'll figure it out, honey. You always do. Maybe you should take the week off and just stay here."

"I can't do that."

"How much sick leave do you have built up?"

Natalya was never sick and they both knew it. They owed her for weeks of time—it would be months, except sick leave didn't roll over year to year. She *could* log in from here for critical meetings…

"Next weekend is Stormy Days at Eagle Cove—Jessica's latest promotion for the town. Everyone could use an extra hand. You call in sick and we'll go from there."

"I…" Could she? "I've never done anything like that."

"Well," her mother patted her briskly on the back which told Natalya that the hug was now over. "What you're going to do now is sit down while I cook breakfast and all of us will figure it out together. Okay?"

"I guess," Natalya felt as if she was twelve again. "Who is 'all of us together'?"

Her mom just patted her back again, whispered, "Surprise!"

And let her go.

Natalya opened her eyes and looked over her mother's shoulders, straight into Cal's eyes. He sat at the table, to her back as she'd gone for the coffee. An empty mug was clenched in his big hand.

"Hey there, Gnat."

# # #

"Hey there?" Natalya's voice came out as a tight squeak.

He shrugged. "Don't really know where else to go with it, Gnat."

"You could have said something when I came in the room."

"Like what?" He could see her building up a head of steam, but didn't know how to defuse it. Though he did figure it wasn't quite the right moment to point out that her robe had slipped open enough for him to tell that she wore neither t-shirt nor bra.

"Like, oh, I don't know. How about, 'Hey, Gnat.' Would that have killed you?"

"Not a problem, if I could have spoken." Because sleepy-eyed, elk-slippered, and wrapped in a terrycloth bathrobe as dark as her eyes, she'd knocked the wind right out of him. Twice he'd gotten to hold her and wake up beside her. And it wasn't until this moment that he understood quite how amazing and unusual a gift that was for a big lummox like himself.

"Don't see your muzzle, Mad Dog Mason. Seems to me you could have spoken just fine." She was up on her toes and leaning toward him. In a moment he'd find out if she was wearing underwear under that robe or not.

"Kinda *like* that." He wasn't going to give her the satisfaction of the truth that she could steal his voice as well as having filled every waking thought for the last two weeks. "Mad Dog? Yeah! It works. Though Mad Baker might be more accurate."

And she growled just as dangerously as one.

"Sit down, Gnat."

"Or what?" Except for the thin line of the belt and an equally thin line of black cotton behind it, he now had a clear view that went from her ridiculous slippers, all the way up one impossibly long leg, a curve of hip he remembered—that dip just inside the hip bone that fit the stroke of his thumb so well—and clear up to her throat showing his kind of cleavage.

Cal grinned, he couldn't help himself. "Or at least close your robe before I'm forced to throw you over my shoulder and drag you upstairs."

She looked down, cursed as her mother turned around in time to see and unleash one of her big laughs, then Natalya yanked it tighter around her neck than a formal kimono.

"Now will you sit down?" He did his best to sound as if he was coaxing a three-year old.

She didn't miss that and looked around for some other option, but apparently didn't find it so she dropped down onto the other bench seat of the small breakfast booth. Even when pissed she moved with a smooth grace that was a miracle to watch. It had him shifting in his seat trying to get comfortable without being obvious about his body's reaction in front of a couple women.

Gina set Natalya's abandoned coffee mug on the table along with one of the chocolate-filled croissants Cal had brought with him as a bribe to get Natalya's phone number. Gina rested a warm hand on Cal's shoulder and squeezed encouragingly.

"A word of advice for the future, she's always snippy until she's eaten something."

"Mom! Not true. Besides, Cal does not need to know things 'for the future.'" But Cal noted that her fingers were ignoring her protests and had already torn off a bite-sized piece of the croissant.

Gina squeezed his shoulder again and returned to the stove and her breakfast prep.

"What are you doing here, Mason?"

Grab the bull by the horns? Sure, he liked living dangerously. "Looking for you."

"No, you weren't." A second bite disappeared fast after the first.

"Sure. Thought I'd…" but among things he didn't want to reveal was that once he'd gotten her phone number, he'd been planning to drive to Portland before calling it. Then he'd seen her MINI Cooper parked out front and been prepared to haunt the B&B's kitchen all day if necessary. "…I'd see if you were around and wanted to go for a walk or something."

She turned to glare out the window. The Coast's changeable weather was favoring him at the moment and a quiet sunrise was occurring beneath clear skies. She might be upright, and vibrating with emotions, but she wasn't awake yet. In a few more minutes she'd be awake enough that so simple an evasion wouldn't have succeeded but he'd take what he could get for the moment.

"Beautiful morning out there," he prompted.

"No, you didn't come here for a walk."

"Okay, Ms. Telepathic Lamont, why *am* I here?" He went for more coffee because her robe was slipping open about the neck again and he really needed to adjust some things. And getting coffee also gave him a moment to keep his own balance.

"You're here because you want me to be your sex kitten this weekend."

He poured slowly, trying to find a way to breathe despite that image slamming into his nervous system. Her mother's sly, sideways smile at him didn't help matters. He took his time walking back to the table.

"Maybe," he nodded thoughtfully as he sat then sipped his coffee. "At least that was the initial plan. But I think your mom's right, she's a smart woman."

"I am!" Gina declared. He'd noted that she was working her pans and the big griddle particularly quietly so that she wouldn't miss a word. "About what?"

"Yes, about what, Mad Baker Mason?"

"I think you should definitely call in sick."

"So that I can be your sex kitten for the whole week instead of just a weekend?"

"Well," he made a point of glancing down at her chest.

She followed his gaze and snatched her robe closed again. Damn but he could spend a whole lot of time teasing Natalya Lamont and counting it all as well spent.

"No. I was thinking that you could do something other than that."

"Like what?"

"Not sure. I mean at some point we'll have to sleep, I suppose."

"Someone save me," she cast her glance to the heavens, or at least the kitchen's ceiling. Thankfully, she'd kept a hand clamped around the neck of her robe which was the only thing saving him at the moment.

She finished her coffee and croissant in silence, all one-handed.

He took the time to appreciate sitting with her as the rich smells of a B&B breakfast filled the kitchen. Frying bacon, individual salmon quiches in the oven, and strawberry smoothies made with fruit Gina had put up in the freezer fresh-picked at the height of the summer season.

Again he was having problems.

Sure he wanted to bed Natalya, because talk about the best sex ever…whew! He just *had* to find out if that was all real or merely his imagination.

But he'd also woken up alone for two full weeks and caught himself each time reaching to see if she was beside him. And he still hadn't washed the pillowcase she'd slept on the night of the weddings when they hadn't had sex. He was eight kinds of pitiful; there was no way it could still smell like her, but he kept imagining that it did.

He had it bad and couldn't figure out how he was going to take care of that. Unless the next time they had sex it was awful, but even then he'd—

"Do you still run?"

Cal shrugged. "Not like when I was in school. But yeah." A baker had to do something or he'd turn into the size of two bakers. Since he was starting out at six-four with a Swedish farmhand build, it wouldn't be a pretty sight. And just breathing the air could be fattening in the Blackbird.

She leaned over to look under the table. "In those shoes?" Her bathrobe, forgotten again, slid open as she did and his blood pressure which had been spinning down skyrocketed back up.

"Good as any."

"Okay, give me a couple minutes."

Natalya rose and headed out of the kitchen, her bathrobe sliding off one shoulder. No, she hadn't forgotten about it for a moment. At the doorway, just before she disappeared up the shadowed stairs, she glanced back at him over her shoulder. The motion caused her bathrobe to practically slide off one whole side, exposing her shoulder, waist, one cheek of her butt, and the back of her leg all the way down to her brown fuzzy slippers.

That's when Cal caught sight of that smile of hers.

Then she was gone.

"Holy mother of god," Cal flopped against the back of the bench seat and rubbed his eyes.

Right. Natalya had always been the dangerous one.

Her mother's knowing smile wasn't helping him at the moment.

# # #

Natalya checked the mirror and decided that revenge was such a fun game. She'd see how Cal survived this morning's run. He may "still run" but in Portland she'd taken it back up with a vengeance.

Six months ago, despite a slightly dirty head start on Natalya's part, Jessica had outrun her by three paces for the prize of breakfast at the Puffin Bay Diner—exactly as Jessica had done to her at their final high school meet, though that had been a fair start and the prize had only included a cheap blue ribbon and bragging rights. And she could still remember just how much mileage her cousin had gotten out of the second part of that prize.

After half a year of running almost every day, Natalya figured she could run Jessica into the ground, even if she wasn't four months pregnant.

Cal was about to get an education.

She trotted down the stairs in her running gear. Skin tight and lime green swirled with dark chocolate brown. Her Nikes, from a trip with a former boyfriend (who liked to pretend they'd get back together someday even though he knew they weren't) to the Nike campus employees' store. Wrap-around shades. Her hair back in a ponytail. Cardio band on one wrist; Mace spray on the other. She'd left her music player behind since she'd be running with someone. Well, at least briefly, until she'd dusted him on the trail.

Natalya stepped into the kitchen and suddenly had a challenge of her own.

Cal had a gym bag at his feet; it must have been in his Vette. He still wore a close-fitting turtleneck, but he'd pulled on runner's shorts. His legs were massive, powerful pistons that looked like they should be bolted into the earth, except he was dancing lightly on his toes, warming up. Instead of beat-up tennies, he wore a pair of ASICS.

He looked her up and down once, very slowly, which didn't harm her ego any. All he'd be seeing after this was her backside.

"Who you gonna Mace, Gnat?" He tried to sound casual but she could hear the roughness in his voice as he struggled with her body-hugging outfit.

"A rabid seagull, a porpoise with a foul purpose…maybe a Mad Dog," she shrugged. "You never know what you'll find around here."

Mom breezed into the kitchen with an empty tray and began filling it with quiches. "Just don't Mace him in my kitchen. I have guests."

Natalya peeled the canister off the Velcro patch and tossed it on the counter. Then they shifted out onto the porch to finish their stretching.

The sun was up now, though not high enough to light more than the tops of the ridge. It wouldn't clear the Coast Range for another ten or twenty minutes. And the high bluff bank would shade the beach for a couple more hours.

But the morning was a fine one. Mid-forties, the air had a nice freshness to it without the sharp snap of thirties. And there was no taste of snow on the air.

Watching Cal stretch and warm up was backfiring on her plan to make him suffer. If it went on much longer, she'd be the one to suffer. In silent consent they headed off the porch and finished their warmup with a slow side-by-side start.

Cal started for the stairs down to the beach, but Natalya turned instead for the slender track up to the lighthouse. LBB Lane was paved from the town out to the two grand Victorians at the end of town: the Slaters where the Judge and now Peggy lived in the main house with Jessica and Greg in the guest house, and the Lamont B&B. Past her mom's house, the unpaved one-lane wound up the side of Orca Head, twisting through the thick trees. It was driven only once or twice a month by service personnel checking on the automated light and Marty the town cop drove up there a couple times more. It was a common stop for outdoor teenage adventure—Natalya had certainly led a few boys astray up here—but as long as you were discreet and didn't leave any garbage behind, Marty didn't seem to mind.

Natalya used to run up here all the time in high school for the workout, but it had been years. The gravel was hard-packed in the tire tracks, though tall grasses grew between them. It made her glad of her leggings, which got damp from the grass, but Cal's bare legs were soon dripping with water.

It was only half a mile up to the light, but it switchbacked twice and maintained a stiff grade. Her legs could definitely feel it as they wound through towering conifers and scrub oak. The forest was alive with complaints at these strange two-footed intruders. Squirrels scrambled up vertical trunks then chittered at them from high branches. Stellar jays swooped over to see who was interfering and dozens of little brown birds, flitting too fast to be identified, shot aloft.

Thankfully Portland was built against the base of the Tualatin Mountains which had been preserved as a five thousand acre park. Less than ten blocks out her apartment door lay seventy miles of forested trails. It was perfect for a former cross-country team co-captain. Cal's workouts for soccer in high school had been mostly sprints and flat track work, so this was another edge in her favor.

They burst out of the trees at the old lighthouse keeper's cottage and stopped to look. The cottage itself had seen better days but offered a commanding view both north and south. It sat at the end of the woods a hundred feet shy of the light itself.

To the north, Eagle Cove trailed along the beach from the B&B two miles up to the mouth of the Eagle River where the bay met the ocean. Beyond that was untenanted forest land, no neighbors just across the bay. To the south, tall sea crags dotted the shoreline. Small cove beaches, accessible only by boat, and more forest. The next town was invisible around a point less than ten miles away, but would take thirty miles to reach by road.

The rocky clearing was dominated by the three-story tall lighthouse. In the quiet morning she could just hear the soft whir of the motor that spun the stepped Fresnel lens which cast its guiding light out to sea. Actually, it wasn't a guiding light. It was a "Caution! Do not approach!" light. The guiding lights were small flashing green and red beacons marking the channel into Eagle Bay.

"Interesting choice, Gnat." Cal was still trotting in place to keep warm. Here atop the bluff they were in the first sunlight of the day to reach the coast and it was warm against her face.

"Why?"

"Well," he nodded toward the base of the light. "Might have lost my virginity to Allyson Chaney right over there."

"Allyson? Really?" She'd been one of those purer than bleached cotton types that Natalya had never understood, always looking down on everyone who wasn't as pristine as she was.

"Oh yeah," Cal sounded far too pleased with his memory of the experience.

It was also uncomfortably close to where she and Nicky Vance had their first, then second and final times together.

"Well, isn't that amusing." Cal read her far too easily. And the changing shape of both his smile and his running shorts showed exactly where his thoughts were going.

"Not a chance, Mason." She turned to follow the trail that led up into the logging roads—and nearly flattened Tiffany. They both yelped in surprise at the narrowly avoided collision.

Tiffany was dressed far more sensibly than either of them. She wore her usual battered hiking boots and jeans. She also wore a warm jacket and a Bohemian wide-brimmed floppy hat that would shed rain, block sun, and made her face a little difficult to see as she was several inches shorter than Natalya. Her long brown hair was in a French braid flipped to the front so that it wouldn't be caught in the heavy backpack she wore.

"Not many people come up here. At least not in the winter." As usual, she spoke barely loud enough to be heard. Every conversation she'd ever had with Tiffany required leaning in to be sure to hear her soft words. Up here, with the wind blowing up over the bluff and the cry of a pair of seagulls soaring on it, her voice seemed doubly soft.

Natalya had forgotten that Tiffany had homesteaded somewhere up here in the forest. Since her boyfriend had bailed on her and taken her truck with him, she'd remained aloof and alone out here in the wilderness. She only came to town for knitting days and to sell her produce in town, always afoot no matter the weather. She probably couldn't afford to replace the missing truck.

"We're just out for a run."

Tiffany tipped her head up enough for her gray eyes to become visible. "You don't seem to be running."

"We stopped for a moment to admire the view," Cal spoke as if to a child.

But Natalya knew from past experience that Tiffany's comments might sound stupid at times, but that she was actually very sharp and missed nothing.

"The view is best on the other side of the light," and she offered one of her enigmatic smiles to Natalya as if she'd been there fifteen years ago to see exactly where Natalya had given herself to Nicky.

Then Tiffany turned and started down the trail toward town.

"She's right you know," Cal said. "She's strange, but right. Let's go see."

"Not interested in revisiting the site of your old conquests, Mason." Nor her own. She bounced on her toes a couple of times and headed for the trail that climbed up into the woods.

"Nothing wrong with making some new conquests there," Cal grumbled, but fell into step close behind her.

# # #

Natalya must be part mountain goat and part jackrabbit. She ran as fast up steep trails as she did down them. But she was giving him a fine motivation for keeping up, because her running togs hid almost nothing other than the color of her skin. Many women he'd seen in tight leggings really shouldn't go there—but the whole concept had been designed with women like Natalya in mind.

Women like Natalya. *How many of those have you met, Mason?*

Could count them on one finger and her name was Natalya Lamont.

She set a pace that excluded conversation. A couple of times she'd tried opening up the lead on him. The first time she'd added a dozen paces before he'd caught on and closed the gap. After that, he hung solid, three paces back.

He might be breathing too hard to talk, but he could still think. It had taken a mile past the lighthouse before he managed to think about something other than her body. The image of taking her up against the lighthouse with only ocean and sky as witnesses was a very powerful one.

But somewhere in the second mile he also started thinking about the sleepy-eyed woman he'd watched this morning. The one that had left him unable to speak when faced with that unexpectedly quiet and serene version of Natalya.

Only not so serene.

Her tears may have discomfited her mother, but it had left him with a lot to think about.

I don't even know what's wrong.

About the only thing he could think of that was wrong with his life was that he wasn't curled up in a bed with Natalya at the moment. He liked baking. There was a sameness to each day's tasks, but there was art there as well—what baked right one time might not work the next. Baking was advanced chemistry, a class he'd done particularly well in because of that understanding.

The business was taking off well enough that he'd had the extra cash to buy the Corvette outright. He had poker buddies, the occasional lover, and afternoons and weekends off to enjoy the beach, get in some fishing, or go for a run. He and Dad shared dinner as often as not. Cal had never had big dreams and was doing fine with that.

They hit a logging road that led back down toward town, and Natalya picked up the pace. He leaned into the run to keep up with her, but didn't try pulling alongside because he knew that would just goad her on. With the way she looked running, as graceful as if born to it, he wondered if just maybe she could dust him.

There were others like him who were doing well here: Vincent building fine furniture out of his garage, Becky and her brewery, Dad, Gina Lamont, the list went on.

Some had big, out-in-the-world dreams. But it was as if they were coming home to roost. The Judge had never left, though he'd commuted to Newport for thirty years before staying home and opening the diner. Harry had been a hot-shit New Orleans lawyer for a decade before coming back to take his father's place on the bench. Greg's high-end restaurant, open only on Friday and Saturday nights, was good enough he could have made a go of it anywhere. But he hadn't; he'd opened it in Eagle Cove.

Jessica was in yet another category. Her journalism career had collapsed along with the newspapers. She was now the town's marketing guru and kicking ass at it—just as you'd expect from Jessica. He really needed to talk with Dad about bringing on some help before the summer because if the tourism kept picking up at the rate Jessica had it increasing, they'd need it.

Then there was Natalya, who had shifted up the pace another notch. Thankfully his body enjoyed the view and had kept close while his thoughts wandered. Though if she took it much faster, she just might leave him behind.

Natalya's career was rocking. He looked up her company online in the two weeks he'd spent trying not to think about it. Their backdated press releases announced any number of new clients, the employment opportunities listing was long, and Natalya was often mentioned in the newsletters.

Yet she'd wept on her mother's shoulder this morning.

I don't even know what's wrong.

Yeah, he'd really like to have Natalya in his bed for a whole week—his initial reason for agreeing that she should call in sick. But he'd bet there were other reasons too. More important ones.

"Hey, Gnat. I think—" he started to speak to her, but she wasn't there. She'd slipped away once they'd hit the up and down hills of Gull Way. He spotted her half a block ahead, kicking hard as she turned onto Shearwater Lane. They hadn't called a finish line, but she was going after it like she had one in mind.

Cal dug in and sprinted hard. He blew by Vincent's, not even bothering to wave a hand at the shouted greeting. Besides, Vincent had finished in the money last night, going home fifteen dollars heavy—Cal had to hold a grudge on that for at least a day.

By the end of Shearwater, she was still way out in front. Along Egret Hollow he gained a little ground. She skipped Sandpiper Circuit, but now he guessed at her direction. He took the turnoff, but didn't follow the second half of the circuit. Instead, he raced through Andrea Martin's landscaping business (clearing several rows of blueberry bushes like a line of hurdles), shot across Beach Way, through Sleepy Owl Hotel's parking lot, and came at her sideways on the sandy beach.

"Cheater!"

He swung in close beside her. Two miles to her mother's B&B. It would be a hard race, and a good one. But her mom was there and had a houseful of guests. He wanted Natalya to himself.

Cal squeezed in on her, edging her toward the water. In a hundred yards he had her dancing along the edge of the surf without realizing it. Then he did a move he'd perfected on the soccer field. He made as if to stumble and turn abruptly while actually pushing just a little ahead. Without any contact, no illegal pushing of the opponent, he used her own instinctive reaction to make her stumble into the ocean to avoid his pretended fall.

"Goddamn it, Mas—"

That's when he tackled her.

Full body hug, he threw them both into an oncoming wave, though he did twist to take the brunt of the fall himself.

"What the—" the breaking wave crashed over her face and left her gasping and sputtering out sea water.

"Sorry, Gnat. Guess I tripped." When the icy water dragged back to sea they were both drenched through and sitting in only about six inches of water.

A husky, who'd been romping in and out of the waves after a Frisbee, rushed over to see what was happening. He shook his coat off in their faces, then bounded away to his owner's call.

Cal wiped the water off his face. "Gotta get me one of those someday," he teased her, wishing his life was a little different so that he actually could. It wouldn't be fair to lock a big dog up while he was in the bakery all day.

"Great! Then I can always smell like wet dog. I knew I should have brought my can of Mace."

"You wouldn't Mace some poor dog?"

"Never! But you I'd spray in a heartbea—"

He rolled her down into the next wave just for the hell of it.

"Now you don't smell of wet dog anymore," he said when they resurfaced. "Besides, I thought you might be overheated from your run."

"Well now I'm freezing!"

"I know a place close by where we can go to get warm."

She glanced up the beach. "You should be hung, drawn, quartered, and hung again!" But she was grinning at him. His apartment was only one block over.

The next wave had her leaping out of his grasp, pushing off hard against his shoulder to get clear. Unable to make it back to his own feet in time, the icy wave drove into his face and knocked him flat. It also dragged a massive load of sand up his shorts.

# # #

The bottom of the tub was all gritty beneath her feet. It seemed no matter how much Cal rinsed, there was more sand to be found. Her hair was an unruly snarl of seawater and sand as well.

One moment they were giggling and washing each other like a couple of children beneath the steaming spray. The next moment Cal had her back slammed up against the shower wall, his body pressed hard against her, his face just an inch from hers.

"I've got an awful need for you, Lamont." But he didn't take. No matter how badly he wanted, he didn't take.

She brushed her fingers over his cheek. The image of sex out at the lighthouse had gotten planted deep in her brain by Tiffany's knowing smile. And then to have Cal pace her through a half dozen miles as if he was her shadow only heightened the thought until the image had become a searing need. She'd waited long enough for the idea to plant itself distractingly deep in Cal's thoughts as well and then pulled away by stretching out her stride without changing the speed of her steps. People always fell for that trick. They'd match her pace, until it was like a metronome to them. That's when she'd stretch out her long legs—a trick which had won her any number of races. Only Jessica never fell for that, as her cousin's legs were just as long as Natalya's.

And Cal had decided that race be damned, he wanted her more than he wanted to win.

His blue eyes were watching her, desperate with need. He was taking no advantage despite having pinned her to the wall. She could push him away with no more pressure than to move a feather. He made it clear that the choice was hers, that the power was hers.

That was a heady tonic she couldn't resist.

As she pulled his head down into a kiss, Natalya wondered if he knew that. Even if he was manipulating her, it was to right where she wanted to be.

Chapter 9

*N*atalya lay alone on Cal's big bed listening to Hank Williams crooning out *Jambalaya*. She felt both wrung out and thoroughly energized.

They'd woken to *American Pie* which she'd argued really shouldn't be on his list because it wasn't about food. He'd mumbled in between her breasts—his favorite place to wake up—that even songs about food were mostly about other things. ABBA came on next with *Honey, Honey* to prove his point. When he'd tried to leave to go bake, she'd pulled him back and they'd had that quickie he so wanted, to Maroon 5 belting out *Sugar*. Though they'd finished to The Monkees' *Tapioca Tundra* which had them groaning for multiple reasons.

Two days. Despite her protestations, she had spent two straight days being Cal's sex kitten. Of course he'd been a sex *god* so it was hard to complain. It hadn't all been sex, but they hadn't gone out either. As predicted, they'd slept some. They'd watched a couple of Jason Bourne action movies while eating delivery pizza on the sofa. And they'd taken turns reading aloud chapters of the latest Lee Child thriller—after all, Cal was built on the scale of Jack Reacher and she'd ad-libbed certain lewd comparisons as she read.

Now it was Monday.

Time to leave her little two-day idyll and start thinking again.

First, she'd have to go home and get some clothes. All she had here was her running togs. For the entire weekend, when she'd worn clothing, it had been nothing but a big shirt that declared "Bakers Do It With Chocolate"—a truth Cal had very thoroughly proven upon her willing body. And he'd left her this morning with an evil grin while wearing a "Darth Baker" t-shirt, though she'd kept her butt safely under the covers so that he didn't smack it again in his glee.

Second, she'd have to decide about taking the week off "sick." Within the next hour she either needed to get in her car and drive, or call in. And she needed to make the decision on her own before her mother had a chance to argue her point once again. Mom was such a primal force that Natalya had learned—shortly after childbirth probably—that she had to make the really important decisions on her own.

This week's schedule was—

Even thinking about the office made her feel a bit ill.

She flopped face down as Harry Belafonte broke into *The Banana Boat Song (Day-O)*. It was the same position she'd been in two weeks ago on Monday morning: her bones just as liquid as they were now, her face once again buried in Cal's pillow which smelled mostly of him and, this time, a little bit of chocolate.

She wasn't going to call in sick just so that she could keep having amazing sex.

Tempting, but no.

Again the thought of going to work…

Her gut clenched.

Well, if she didn't want to go to work, then what did she want?

That answer wasn't forthcoming as she dressed and made the bed.

She didn't find it going down the stairs either.

At the bottom, the door into the bakery was open. She turned in.

Cal was there, of course, like a hulking demon in his laboratory. The bright worklights made the floating flour dust sparkle in the air as he smacked a bread loaf. Sugar, jam, and, yes, chocolate assaulted her nose. He stood before a great counter of stainless steel working methodically down the row kneading massive balls of dough, slapping them with flour, and setting them aside to keep rising. Behind him, the big ovens were heating up.

She watched him for a long time before speaking. He was so beautiful. His big muscles rippling as he manipulated bags of flour and giant mixers, turning out giant piles of dough. He was power embodied, but also finesse. She could watch him all day.

"Everything in your world is so orderly, Mason."

He didn't jolt. Cal simply looked up at her and smiled. He brushed his hands together releasing a puff of flour. "Baking is an orderly process otherwise it doesn't work."

"I'm rather envious." Because her world, that looked so orderly from the outside, was a screwed up mess inside her head. A mess she couldn't seem to get a handle on. She only knew that it hurt.

Cal came around from behind his counter. He paused a moment to look her up and down, with that lusty smile she'd come to know so well.

"Not helping, Cal."

"Sorry, Gnat. But you are an incredible sight in or,"—he leered—"out of your running gear." Then his expression sobered. "And the gift you've given me these last two days, well, it's something that just makes a guy happy."

"I suppose," she saw the hurt at her vague response as soon as she said it. She placed a hand on the middle of his chest. "No, Cal. Don't go there. You're all a woman could ask for and then some. And I'm sorry that I'm a damned bitchy one at four in the morning."

"Can I get you something to eat?" His smile was a teasing reminder of her mother's instructions to him, but she could still see the hurt there that she hadn't repaid the compliment. She searched inside but couldn't find anything to say.

"No. I just need to get home."

Cal went cautious, "Home here or home Portland?"

"I don't know yet."

He nodded slowly. "Let me give you a ride home in the van." Both the Vette and her MINI were still at the B&B.

"Your dough," she waved a hand toward the table.

"I can spare ten minutes."

She nodded, didn't know what else to do. It would be a long cold walk in her tights and she was sick to death of running. Especially when she didn't know if she was running away or running toward something.

# # #

Cal drove the delivery van slowly, giving Natalya time to think, but she still hadn't said a word. He finally understood that if he didn't speak, no one would.

"Hey, Gnat?"

"Yes, Cal," she sighed in a tolerant tone. He debated but decided that it was best to keep using her nickname.

"As a friend, not as the guy who loves having you in his bed…"

"Uh-huh?" her tone was carefully noncommittal.

He slowed the truck at the Slater's, finally pulled over and doused the headlights, but left the engine and heater running. Was he about to step over some line? They'd spent an entire weekend together and not once talked about anything important. Not a single word.

"What, Cal?"

"I just think," he turned to look at her shadowed face barely lit by the B&B's porch light filtering through the thin line of trees that separated the properties. "I think you really should call in sick. Not to spend with me, though you know I wouldn't mind that."

"Wouldn't *mind?*"

"Okay, a part of me is down in the footwell," he thumped his sneaker on the van's floor for emphasis, "trying to sell his soul to the Devil to get you to stay with me." There wasn't quite enough light to tell if that earned him a smile or not.

"And the other part?"

"The other part thinks his friend Natalya should take some time for herself. Some time to think about this last weekend."

"This weekend was all about sex, Cal. Awesome sex, but that's all it was."

"That's my point. I'm gone on you, Gnat, you know that. You want to shack up and never leave, I'll be a happy man. But all weekend you didn't say a single word about what had you crying on your mom's shoulder. Never seen you cry before, Gnat."

"I—" her voice choked off. "I don't do it much, Cal."

"Well, something's in there. If you go back to Portland, you'll get busy as hell and not think about it. I'm just saying maybe you should hang out here. See me or don't. But you ripped us both apart with that weeping. You're so goddamn amazing, neither of us knows where that came from."

"That makes three of us. I don't know either, Cal. Not that it's any comfort."

He reached out and took her hand which was far colder than could be accounted for by the bakery van's lame heater. "That's my point."

Natalya remained still and silent, but did squeeze his hand back when he squeezed hers before he let go.

"I'll drop you off now; my dough can't wait much longer. But if you need to talk, you let me know. Call me from Portland and I can be there in three hours. Okay?"

No response.

"Okay?"

"Yeah. Thanks, Cal. You're the best. In many ways."

He dropped the van into gear and drove around the last clump of trees. He didn't hit the headlights because he didn't want them to shine in some sleeping guest's window at four-thirty in the morning.

On the porch in the glow of the porch light was a sight unlike anything he'd ever seen.

Gina Lamont stood there, her bathrobe wide open where she was pressed against a man that she was kissing hard. The man's arms were inside the robe, clearly holding her close.

Then they turned in unison to face his van.

"Dad?"

# # #

Natalya and Cal Sr. nodded cautiously at each other as they crossed paths at the bottom of the steps. Senior moved to the van driver's window as Natalya stepped up onto the porch.

"Close your robe, Mom."

"What? Oh." She wore a light cotton nightgown underneath the robe…very light and quite short. It didn't hide anything about her mother's generous figure. "Sorry. I'm just a bit…"

"Breathless?"

"Yes."

Natalya wasn't sure if she'd ever seen her mother made fluttery by a man before.

Together they turned to watch the two Cals. The men spoke too softly to be overheard, so Natalya decided to fill in the script.

"Hi, Dad," Natalya did her best to imitate Cal Jr.'s deep voice, though she kept it to a whisper so only her mother would overhear.

"Hey, Junior," her mother answered in kind, imitating Cal Sr.

"See you at the bakery?" Natalya offered as both men looked away from one another.

"Sure, son," her mother finished. And that must have been fairly accurate, because Cal Sr. turned on his heel and clambered into his pickup.

Cal didn't move. Natalya could feel him looking at her. She'd known and hadn't told him. She'd figured it was her mother and his father's business, but now she wished she had.

She raised a hand, but didn't see an answering one before he backed in a half circle, turned on the headlights, and headed into town. Moments later Cal Sr. was gone as well.

"Did yours wave?" Natalya asked her mom.

"Not sure. But he did a few other very nice things."

"Too much information, Mom."

"Anything you want to be telling me?"

"No."

"Stingy!" Then her mom laughed, though quietly because of the guests, as they entered the kitchen. "Bet you twenty dollars the two of them spend the whole morning baking together and never say a word about it."

Natalya smiled. "No bet." And then her smile slipped away. Wasn't that what Cal had just pointed out to her, that she hadn't shared a thing about herself? But if she had, she just might have started crying again and that wasn't going to solve anything. And if it started again, she was half afraid that she wouldn't be able to stop. For now she'd keep her peace and head up to her room.

Three hours later, that's where she still was. Sitting on the foot of her bed, watching the walls as the darkness outside began lightening toward day.

At eight, she pulled out her phone and called in sick with a bad flu. Dan's sympathy, and telling her to just lie low and get better because he'd handle any meetings that came up, didn't make her lie sit any better. But she truly didn't feel up to the long drive back to Portland.

By nine, sunlight was poking over the Coast Range and the first squares of brilliant yellow were slipping through the south window. The first thing they lit was her demon sketch from that day in the woods, or at least the final evolution of the idea. Cal might no longer be recognizable in the finished work, but she saw him there nonetheless.

The demon who was doing strange things to her. The demon who looked like a magician in his bakery and like…she didn't know what…as he rode down upon her until they were both writhing with the pleasure of it.

Natalya went to the footlocker that any guest would assume was merely decorative. She reached around the back and took the key off the tiny hook there. Inside, beneath the iron-banded wooden lid, were her art supplies: a roll of canvas, palette, paints and pastels, a stack of various-sized sketchbooks, folded-up easel, and a couple of stretched canvases.

She didn't need to start with a pencil. The picture had been so clear in her head over these last two days.

Natalya started with the brown acrylics.

First, the poker table.

Chapter 10

*W*ell, at least Cal now knew where Dad had gotten his "energy" two weeks before. When he recalled a stray comment from Natalya, Cal almost punched a hole in the pie dough he was rolling out for Scottish pasties intended for lunch service.

He woke up full of energy, Cal had said.

Or he never went to sleep, Natalya had declined to clarify her mumble.

And Dad had commented about seeing Natalya driving his Corvette. But Dad didn't live on LBB Lane. When he'd given Cal sole possession of the apartment for a high school graduation present, he'd bought a small place out on Gull Way, not far from the airport.

Cal's first instinct was to be pissed. At Natalya. At his father.

Even if Natalya had decided it was none of *her* business, it was his father and that was part of *his* business. Except, it really wasn't. Senior had just as much right to his privacy as Cal did. Hell, Cal and Natalya had just spent two full days in a love nest right upstairs while his father ran the bakery Saturday.

Still didn't sit quite right.

"Sleep much?" Cal couldn't stop himself.

"Not a wink," Senior was clearly bragging as he rolled out the bagel dough and started bending it into circles. "You?"

"Not much," then he knew how to get back at his father for all of those times he'd caught the bigger salmon, snagged the bigger burger, or found the better deal in a flea market. "Of course, it was two straight days and nights. Had to sleep a little."

His Dad just nodded and stayed focused on his bagels, but still it felt good.

# # #

When six hit, they had the bagels boiled and baking in the oven.

Cal headed over to the diner. No sign of either car. But the diner wasn't empty even right at six. Cal was always first in as the doors were unlocked. Excitement rose—until he saw that it was Jessica, not Natalya, sitting at the counter.

The Judge was back in place in the kitchen and Greg was running the front of house again.

Cal dropped down on his stool, "The usual."

Greg wrote it up just that way ("The usual"), put it in the spinner rack, and slapped it around. The Judge immediately set a fully dressed tall stack of pancakes on the service ledge and pulled down the order slip. It was all ritual now between the three of them, had been for a long time. Cal liked the comfort of it. The steadiness.

"Hey, Jess."

"Hey, Giant." She didn't have a meal in front of her. Instead she had notebooks and printouts and was scribbling notes on a pad.

"What's all that?"

"Stormy Days at Eagle Cove."

"Oh, when's that?"

"When's that?" Jessica spun to face him. "When's that!" She now had Greg and the Judge's full attention. "It's in five goddamn days, Mason! I've been working on it for three months. I've been giving you updates and timelines for three damn months. You're going to be open this coming Saturday *and* Sunday. Special cupcakes and custom cookies. You're doing a 'Storm Watcher's Box Lunch' if there actually is a storm, a Bird Watcher's one if there isn't. I've already got over a hundred pre-orders for those. I even got Old Man Jaspar at Grouse Hardware to roll over and promise me those individual hand-warmer things—two per lunch order so people can keep both hands warm. You promised me special pastries. You've got to get your shit together, Mason, or I'm going to kill you."

"Oh, that," Cal picked up a piece of bacon and bit down on it. "Yeah, Dad and I have that covered."

"You—" Jessica sputtered.

"Aren't you supposed to be careful about your blood pressure, Jess? You do know you're pregnant, right?" He turned to Greg, but pointed at Jessica with his bacon as he pretended to whisper. "You did tell her she was pregnant, didn't you?"

"Aaaaaaaaa!" Jessica buried her face on her crossed arms.

"Or is it some hormonal thing and you don't want her in on the secret yet?" He kept talking to Greg. "Hope I didn't mess you up, buddy."

Greg rolled his eyes, but he had got the Judge chuckling which was hard to do. He absolutely doted on his two daughters-in-law, but it was clear that he had a special weak spot for Jessica. Besides, Becky was so strong and independent that she was harder to dote on.

Jessica sat up and glared at him. "Next time we'll have *you* be pregnant. We'll start you out with three months of morning sickness and barfing your guts out for breakfast and then see how damned funny you think it all is." She pointed at a plate with a half-eaten piece of dry toast.

"Well, okay. That part doesn't sound so great, but I'm not the one who gets to give birth to a kid and create a new human being."

"Birth. Labor. What a joy *that's* going to be!" She didn't look amused. "I'm going to get you back for this, Mason."

He wasn't worried. It was a pretty empty threat…unless she teamed up with Natalya the evil genius.

The bell on the back of the door rang and Cal spun, but it was the McCalls. Every Monday morning, as a treat before starting their week, Vincent brought all four of them here for breakfast. It was a good thing. Family moment. Nice. Then the twin girls would go off to Dragon Winslow's class, Dawn would be off to try and pound some science into the empty heads of Eagle Cove's high schoolers (his head had sure been empty then of everything except soccer and girls), and Vincent would be back in his garage-shop making furniture.

He glanced out at the lit porch through the big windows. No beautiful woman in a stylish raincoat. Though he saw Hector was already in place by the window with his crossword, Cal hadn't even heard him come in. He'd made Eagle Bay Marina his home for the last three winters, renting a slip for his Pearson 42 sailboat. His biggest fear appeared to be someone getting to the crossword puzzle before he did.

"Hey, Cal," he offered a nod when he noticed Cal looking his way.

"Hey."

"Seven letters. A baker's mistake. Got an 'O' in the middle of her."

"Stupid-ass clue," Cal had heard this one too many times. " 'Bloomer.' It's a UK word for a mistake. Separately, it's a UK word for a really large loaf of bread."

"Gotcha," and he went back to his puzzle. Greg headed over to the McCalls with menus as Cal turned back to his breakfast.

Still no Natalya through the front window.

"So, where's Natalya?" Jessica asked as if she was reading his mind. "I didn't see her all weekend."

"I did. Like every minute for forty-eight straight hours," and the instant he said it he knew it was the wrong thing. What had worked on his dad came out like he was bragging about seeing her when Natalya's best friend and first cousin hadn't. "We spent a fair amount of time together," he went for the backpedal, but knew it was too late.

"And where is she now?"

"Wish I knew. Either at her mom's or halfway back to Portland."

"And you don't know?" Jessica sounded completely disgusted. "How can you say you're in love with her and not know?"

"Look, Jess. I don't like it either. She's trying to deal with some shit and I'm trying to help. She's—" And Cal froze. "Wait! What?"

"Don't try to deny it, Mason, or I'll think less of you than I already do."

"I—" He couldn't deny it, but it wasn't true either. Natalya was amazing. She was far and away the best time he'd ever had. And he hadn't been totally joking when he said he'd be glad to shack up with her long term if she was, you know, in the mood for that. These women were making him into a blithering idiot. He—what? The L-word didn't happen to Mason men, not unless it was spelled L-U-S-T.

His dad and Gina Lamont.

She'd always been the ultra-hot mom of the town with her bright red hair, her tall, amazing figure that had only improved with time, and her infectious laugh. That's what lust looked like, this morning on the porch. The better part of naked, her breasts beneath filmy fabric still rising and falling with her rapid breathing after the kiss Dad had been giving her.

But lust wasn't what he felt for the dark beauty that was her daughter. Not all of it. Maybe not most of it. When she'd waved at him, he'd been unable to respond. Despite the pain that he knew lay below the surface, she had stood so poised, so perfect. No one would ever know she wasn't, except maybe him and her mom. And that's what made her so captivating. She was—

Jessica was still staring at him.

"I'm not confirming or denying shit, Jess."

The bell on the back of the door rang twice more while Jess merely studied him.

"Okay, Cal." And he could see what she was thinking.

"Look," he lowered his voice so that no one would overhear, not even Greg delivering new orders to the window. "Go easy on her, Jessica. She's having a real hard time at the moment. Don't go trying to corner her on shit like…" he shrugged indicating what she'd just done to him. "Right now I think she needs a friend."

"You know what, Mason?" Jessica sat up, patting him on the arm.

"No. What? Maybe I don't want to know what."

"You just might be okay after all."

"Huh." He couldn't think of what to say.

"But don't let it go to your head. Now eat your tall stack and get back to your baking. You've only got five more days."

"It's okay," though he did start eating again. "Dad's helping out this morning."

"On a Monday?" She was local enough to know it was Senior's normal day off.

"Yeah. He and your Aunt Gina were—" And he bit down on his tongue, but again it was too late as Jessica choked and gasped in surprise.

"Your father and my aunt?" She clamped her hand painfully onto his forearm. Her nails weren't long, but she had a strong grip to drive them in with.

He nodded.

"And you and Natalya?"

"We're not a foursome freakshow, Jess."

"No. No. I didn't mean that. But still, it has to be…strange."

Cal nodded. That didn't begin to cover half of it.

# # #

There was a sharp knock on the door that had Natalya jolting. Thankfully she'd just pulled the brush away from the painting to daub up some more cadmium red.

It wasn't her mom's knock, so she just called out, "Go away!" and returned to the painting that had absorbed her attention all morning.

Whoever it was rattled the doorknob, but Natalya had locked the door. She was back to working on Cal's shirt before the footsteps tromped away. Too light to be Cal's, but it didn't matter. She wasn't in the mood to see him either.

The painting had come together so fast. She'd considered moving Cal to the other side of the table so that she could see his face, but that felt too intimate, too personal. Though his face was hidden, he was the dominant figure in the foreground, commanding the canvas. His head was tipped slightly up and back, his joy reflected in the faces of others around the table. She'd shifted the faces so that they weren't recognizable, but anyone who knew Cal would know him in an instant. Her every effort to change that had failed, and she had scraped off and painted over until she'd given in and let him be himself.

She'd also shifted the women's side. The two realities had blended so smoothly: the raucous men's half circle and the quietly peaceful women's half. The rustic bakery and the neatly Victorian parlor.

Except, just to the right of center. There Natalya had placed herself, seated hard against the shadowy disjunction between the two settings. She alone, of all of them, was quiet.

Natalya set down her brush and stared at the painting attempting to puzzle out the expression she'd given herself.

A shadow passed across the sunset's orange light washing into the room—when had it gotten so late? Then a sharp rap on her balcony door had her jumping. She spun to see Jessica opening the door and bringing in a cold blast of air with her.

"Jessica!" Natalya was appalled. She knew exactly the way Jessica had gotten in: climbing the heavy iron mesh from the porch two stories below. The original Lamont daughter had installed it and trained climbing ivy upward to make a home for birds. After a century, it was a thick mass of leaves and vines.

In the spring the ivy wall was so raucous during the day that it was impossible to sleep past sunrise. It had also provided a handy escape for teenage outings which didn't pass by her mother's room.

Jessica looked quite pleased at the surprise she'd just created.

"You're pregnant! You can't be doing things like that!" Natalya rushed over to check on her friend.

"Just four months. I'm not a feeb yet," she pushed away Natalya's hands just as she'd done to Jessica when she was fussing at the wedding. "Greg is already hovering, and Mom asks twice a day if I might want a 'nice lie down.' So don't you start."

Natalya backed off and dropped onto the bed. Jessica did look incredibly healthy. The fair skin of her face pinked by the exertion of the climb. The happy smile that so mimicked the one Natalya had given her in the painting. "You're looking good."

"Just happy I guess." Jessica shrugged. "You'll see when it happens to you."

"A lot of good Greg sex?" Natalya teased going to a subject change. She especially didn't like the appraising look in Jessica's eyes.

"Totally," Jessica sidetracked—at least for the moment. "He's gotten even sweeter since this," and she rested a gentle hand on her own belly.

Jessica had shared, well, entirely too much information during her and Greg's chaotic courtship. Of course she and Jessica had been rooming together at the B&B at the time, so Natalya had been "primary confessor" just as when they were teens. Even from Day One Greg had always been a sweet and gentle lover.

Natalya couldn't help but draw comparisons. Cal wasn't gentle. Not that he was rough, he simply enjoyed sex and threw himself into the act. And sweet was a word she'd never apply. Sex with Cal was an active and energetic exploration of everything that was good. His manners were as frank in the bedroom as they were in public. She glanced over at the painting. He ruled it, though his face was the only one completely hidden. Cal Mason Jr. was emphatically male.

"Hey! This new?" Jessica crossed to the painting.

"Still wet. Don't touch."

Jessica looked at it. And then she went quiet. She stared at it for so long that Natalya's nerves forced her to her feet. Sitting back on the stool in front of the easel, she started to reach for her paints.

"It just needs some—"

"Don't you dare!" Jessica slapped the back of her hand hard enough to sting.

"Ow! What?"

"If you do anything to that painting other than signing your name, I won't speak to you ever again."

"Don't tempt me."

Jessica leaned against her, waist to shoulder, and gave Natalya a sideways hug. Of course she'd know it was an empty threat.

"Really?" It didn't feel finished. Though she couldn't think of what else to do to it. Maybe it was. But it wasn't a comfortable painting.

"Really," Jessica confirmed. "Sign it, now. Before you change your mind."

She stood silently while Natalya took a fine brush and filled in the blocky "N. Lamont" that she'd worked out across the corners of a hundred science- and math-class notebook pages. She circled behind it and knelt to paint her full name and the date on the back of the canvas. After a moment's thought she added, *Joy* and then set down the brush and palette.

"What did you call it?"

"*Joy.*"

"What about her?" Jessica pointed at Natalya's image of herself. She couldn't tell if Jessica didn't recognize Natalya's self-portrait or if Jessica was being kind because the figure didn't fit in with the rest of the painting.

"That's why I wasn't sure if the painting was done. I wanted to make, uh, *her*…happier. But she didn't seem to want to go there."

"Well she's the complete focus of the painting."

Natalya had thought Cal was, dominating the foreground, his head back in laughter.

"It's perfect, Natalya. She's the figure that turns it from a kinda cool painting into an emotional gut punch. The contrast. The ultimate outsider." Then Jessica turned to face her and simply pulled her into a hug and whispered into her ear. "And if that's how you see yourself, you're an idiot."

Natalya held on and Jessica let her. No sob resurfaced. No fiery pain burning in her chest. But over Jessica's shoulder she could see the woman staring quiet-eyed out of the canvas. It was a look she found every morning in the mirror.

# # #

Cal lay in bed wide awake in the dark, second-guessing himself. He knew he'd better get some sleep…but insisting on that wasn't working.

He hadn't gone out to the B&B to see if Natalya was still in town. The Corvette still parked out there had given him the perfect excuse for an afternoon walk, but he hadn't gone. Part of him didn't want to know if she'd left town or not. Another part didn't want to intrude if she hadn't.

He was still fairly certain that Jessica had just been yanking his chain at breakfast, but the question had stuck with him.

Did he love her?

Was he even capable of such a thing? And that was assuming the emotion even existed.

Love wasn't a mother who cheated on her husband with a Corvallis stockbroker and then abandoned her son. But it might be he and Dad baking silently together in the early mornings.

He'd said it to enough women over the years, it seemed to be what they wanted to hear—they'd certainly said it easily enough.

But saying something like that to Natalya Lamont wouldn't be some light, flirtatious, groaned-out-during-sex kind of thing. Around Natalya words were more important, had more meaning. Too bad he didn't know crap about things like that. He'd squeaked out of high school and been glad to be done with the whole mess. His dad and most of his friends hadn't gone to college.

Harry had law school, but Greg only had culinary school. Vincent built great furniture and Alex was learning to be a brewer. Gina Lamont and Jess's parents had never left town for college and were some of the best people he knew.

Maybe Natalya was just having fun with him, because there was no question how much fun they had together; she'd be swept away by some degreed city-boy later. He wasn't inclined to complain about the situation, as he was getting great benefits from it at the moment.

But he didn't much like it either.

Which would make some sense if he was falling—but he wasn't—in love with her. Because love probably didn't even exist…

And shit! He was right back where he'd started.

He yanked the pillow over his face, the one that now very much smelled like Natalya after their two days together, and screamed into it.

Then he froze as he heard a key in the downstairs door. The door opened and closed softly. He pulled aside the pillow and could just pick out the creaking of the stairs as someone ascended slowly. His father's tread would have practically shaken the building, but these steps were light.

He'd left his keys at the B&B when they'd gone for the run and had yet to retrieve them.

The apartment door creaked open and closed again.

Maybe…please…maybe…

"Cal?" the softest whisper in the dark.

"Natalya." The relief breathed out of him with a happy sigh.

Without another word, she moved up beside the bed. He listened to her undress. Scrabbling around on the floor to his side, they had sides now, he found his t-shirt and held it out into the darkness.

She took it from his hand and moments later slipped into the bed beside him. So silently that it was almost as if she wasn't there, she eased against him. Head on his shoulder, her hand resting lightly on the center of his chest, she came to a stop.

"You okay?"

He could feel her uncertain shrug. Cal almost asked if she wanted to talk about it, but suspected that if she wanted to she would. So instead, he kissed her on top of the head and squeezed his arm around her shoulders.

She turned her head enough to kiss his shoulder and then went quiet.

It wasn't long before she fell asleep.

Cal continued to hold her for a long time.

He didn't like the question of whether or not he loved her. However, he was so happy that she had come to him, even in silence, that it didn't really matter. And that thought actually answered the question he was avoiding in the first place.

Which had him smiling.

He considered waking Natalya to tell her, but decided against it. She slept as if exhausted. The morning would give him plenty of time.

The only drawback was that it really sucked that Jessica was right.

So, her he wouldn't tell.

Chapter 11

N*atalya woke to darkness* before the alarm.

Cal wasn't just asleep, he was out. She'd learned the difference during their weekend together. When he was this far under he could sleep through the apocalypse, which would explain why his alarm music was so loud. Maybe that's why she was awake so early, self defense against being alarmed out of her common sense.

That still didn't explain why she was here, because this made no sense at all.

"Just to return his car," had been her excuse to herself as she'd climbed into Cal's Corvette…because naturally that's the most important thing to do at ten at night.

"Merely dropping off his keys," had led her upstairs despite no lights on in the apartment…sure, why not, just stroll into someone's house while he slept.

"For sex," had led her between the covers. Or perhaps that impossible relief she'd heard when he'd whispered her name so hopefully into the dark.

But none of that had turned out to be true.

"To be held!" It had certainly worked. After the wracking exhaustion of creating that painting, it was what she really wanted. To be held. To belong somewhere.

And she had.

Cal had welcomed her without hesitation. Opening his bed and his arms. If he'd asked for sex, she'd have given it. Gladly because she suspected she was a long way from running down Cal's imagination. But somehow he'd known what she really needed and simply let her lie beside him.

Unsure what drove her, she slipped from his bed while he still slept. She had his shirt half off before she changed her mind and pulled it back into place. It was way too big, but it smelled like him.

Tugging on jeans and jacket, she stuffed her bra into the jacket pocket. Unsure how to thank him, she left her own t-shirt on her pillow. It would at least let him know that she wasn't just walking out on him. She tried on one of the hats he had hanging by the door but it dropped down over her eyes and she hung it back up. Rather than trying on any others, she headed out into the night for the two-mile walk home before she could second guess herself back into his bed.

The air was crisp and cool. It smelled of night woods and ocean.

A hat would have been good. She tightened up the front zipper and pulled her hair forward over her ears.

Was she avoiding Cal?

Maybe, if he had started asking things last night, she would be. She wasn't ready for questions yet. Not from Jessica. Not from him. Not from her mother. Hell, she wasn't even ready for them from herself yet.

Where LBB Lane dipped down close to the ocean before climbing back atop the high bluff beach, the background roar of the waves divided into individual crashes on the beach. At any distance, the ocean sounded like a nearby highway. Her Portland apartment was a half-dozen built-up blocks from I-405, but she could still hear the traffic as a deep and steady roar. Similar sounds made by such different worlds.

She could tell the tide was low by how loud the surf was, crashing in on the hard wet sand rather than the softer, quieter sands that had drained dry higher on the beach. Forsaking the road, she followed the moonlight down onto the beach.

The entire length of the beach lay dark but for the lunar nightlight and Orca Head Lighthouse flashing out its warning at the far end of the beach. From Grouse Hardware to the Lamont B&B the entire town slept. She wore no watch and had oddly left her phone at home, so had no way of telling the time. No way to know if Cal had been "alarmed" awake yet and wondering where the hell had she gotten to.

Rather than puzzling at how she felt about doing that to him, the ocean lulled her into not thinking at all as she walked along. Just like Cal had last night. She'd felt so wound up inside, ready to fly apart in a thousand directions at the slightest touch. Yet the moment Cal had wrapped his big arm protectively around her and kissed her atop her head, a peace had washed over her.

She wasn't used to peace.

Portland was about working herself until exhausted, crashing into sleep, then doing it again the next day. When the team went out for drinks—which was a couple times a week—they always hit the hot clubs, and closed them too. Work hard, party hard, pass out hard. That was her life in Portland. In an entire weekend together, she and Cal had each had one beer, because having pizza without beer was just so wrong. But that was it.

Eagle Cove seemed to clear her head of the storms of Portland.

Natalya looked up at the moon. It had a faint glowing ring. Not bright enough to block the brighter stars behind the halo, but it was there. Incoming weather.

She'd have to remember to tell Jessica, she'd be pleased. Maybe her Stormy Days at Eagle Cove festival would bring in some much needed mid-winter business.

Climbing the long flight of stairs up from the beach, Natalya felt as if she was climbing out of the darkness and into the light though it was still hours to sunrise.

At the head of the stairs, she turned and watched the moonlight shining off the foamy wave crests until it looked as if they were glowing. She smelled the air again. A storm *was* brewing out there.

Natalya turned and hurried inside, not even pausing when she saw Cal Sr.'s truck parked out front, except to see if her mother's light was on or off. It was off and the B&B was silent. She wasn't the only one who'd wanted to be held in the quiet of the night.

She tiptoed up to her room and pulled out her biggest canvas. Looking down into the sea chest, she surveyed the possibilities. Oils.

She hadn't worked in oils in years.

# # #

"She's still in town," Cal told Jessica as he sat down beside her.

"Duh!" Jessica didn't even look up from her small laptop. He could see that she was updating the town website that she'd built half a year ago and been expanding ever since.

Greg was waiting expectantly, "The Usual" already written on an order slip.

Cal was half tempted to order an omelette just to screw him up, but that would mean messing with the Judge as well. Finally he just nodded, "Do it."

Greg hung and spun the slip, but rather than simply setting the plate on the ledge, the Judge was watching him carefully. When Cal nodded it was okay, the Judge slid across the tall stack and pulled the ticket. Greg served it across and set the butter and warm maple syrup by his plate bearing bacon and the inevitable hash browns without noticing anything amiss in the "usual" routine.

Jessica might be working, but he could feel her waiting for him to say something more. So he didn't and instead set to eating his breakfast. Besides, he didn't know what to say.

He'd woken up alone, wondering if he'd dreamed her beside him in the night. It wasn't until he was dressing that he spotted her t-shirt over the pillow.

"All women are created equal, but the very best become web designers."

He had a quick mental flash of her walking home naked, then he'd missed his own t-shirt and couldn't help laughing despite his confusion. His had said, "God created man and woman, then he did the hard work and created bakers."

But while he was encouraged by the curious gift, because there was no way he could wear it, he still didn't know what to make of it. Well, now he knew she was in town, he'd just wander out to the B&B after work and maybe find out what was up.

"Not saying much, Giant."

"Not to you, Jess." Passing on Natalya's silence felt good. A little bit of payback in the confusion department.

She eyed him carefully, but didn't argue the point.

Cal finished his breakfast, waved his thanks to the Judge and Greg as he left.

He'd feel a little better if Jessica had looked confused rather than finally nodding as if he finally was doing something right.

# # #

When the knock came on her door this time, Natalya didn't snap at whoever it was to go away—not if there was a chance it would make a pregnant Jessica climb the ivy arbor again.

She called out, "It's open," before she came out of her reverie enough to recognize her mom's knock.

"Oh, you're painting again. That's wonderful, honey."

"Am I?" It didn't feel like she was "painting." It wasn't something she was doing because she liked the process, which she did. The images were simply too clear to keep inside her head. Actually this one was still only part of an image, but it was being too insistent to deny.

"Don't know what else you'd call it," Mom moved closer.

Neither did Natalya, so she didn't argue the point.

She pointed to the *Joy* painting propped on her dresser to distract her mother from the work in progress. Especially because she didn't know where it was progressing to. She dropped her brushes, flipped a cloth over it, and went to stand beside her mother. Natalya glanced out the window and saw that it was early afternoon. She'd been painting since…well, she never had looked at a clock. Since very early.

"That's…" Her mother stopped for a long moment continuing to study the painting. She usually just said, "Oh that's lovely" or the equivalent. She'd long ago confessed that for her, art was mostly about covering empty spots on walls. Which partially explained the B&B.

Every room was heroine-themed by genre.

Natalya had made hers Victorian, but there was the writers' room, kick-ass movie heroines' room, romantic comedies, great woman leaders…ten unique statements about powerful women. But that made the decoration choices simple: mostly framed posters and pictures. She stared at the painting as long as Jessica had yesterday. Then she turned to stare at the walls, cluttered with the best of Natalya's other efforts.

"What are you looking for, Mom?"

"I'm not sure. This one is…different." Natalya had filled in the spaces around the Victorian women in order. She'd started at one side of the bed and worked her way around over the years. It was her progression as an artist.

Natalya tried to study it with a critical eye. There were a few childhood drawings that showed a nice understanding of color if little skill. There had been a dramatic shift when Ma Slater had taken her in hand and given her technique to go with the images in her head. Another change when she'd discovered boys—emotion had taken more of a role. Love found, love lost, and all the chaos of being a teenage girl for sure. But also friendship, solitude, and a host of others.

Then through her twenties the number of paintings had thinned. What there was showed a thoughtfulness, perhaps an over-conscious one. She'd been attempting to manipulate the images to say something she thought was important. That she "thought." The emotional turmoil of her teenage paintings had slowly been filtered out. Steampunk. Traditional Victorian. Studies rather than emotional paintings.

On the wall by the door, her latest, there was a shift back. One she barely recognized as her own. Rather than fantastic settings, she now used more of the Oregon Coast. Sometimes in the foreground, sometimes the background, but it was undeniably here. The emotion had swirled back in on the waves and in the wind. Sometimes it was Victorian set—the pioneer era of the Oregon Coast—sometimes modern. But they were thoughtful portraits of…

"They're all women," her mother exclaimed.

Natalya checked. And almost all of them were, but that wasn't the point. It was—

"That one isn't," once again Mom faced Natalya's latest work.

She'd forgotten how hard it was to complete thoughts around her mother. She'd almost understood something but it had slipped away. It didn't stop her mother from being right. *Joy* wasn't just women. Not with Cal dominating the foreground with his laughter. There was a balance to the image, but—

"That one isn't just lovely, dear. It's powerful, too. I want to be in the group, laughing and enjoying myself, but I also feel that the lone woman in the middle is who I am inside."

"You?" Her mother was one of the most gregarious women on the planet. She'd been born to run a B&B and be the life of the wonderful parties she hosted.

That brought out her mother's big smile, "Me! You captured what it feels like to be a woman, Natalya. That's amazing!"

Natalya stared at her self-portrait again. Maybe "lone" had been the wrong adjective. There was also a peace to the woman.

"Now get out of your t-shirt," for some reason that tickled her mother no end. "It's time to go."

"Go where?" She looked down. She still wore Cal's baking t-shirt. Oversized, comfortable, fallen off one shoulder…and totally ruined. She'd stained it with a dozen dabs of multicolored oils that would never wash out. "Crap! I owe him a new t-shirt."

"Oh, just let him see you wearing it like that now and then and he'll consider himself well repaid. It looks very sexy. As a matter of fact, maybe I should steal one of Cal Sr.'s. Now change."

Suddenly exhausted by her hours in front of the easel, she did as her mother said, first cleaning her fingertips with turpentine and wrapping her brushes in plastic because she knew she'd be back to them soon. "Where are we going?"

"It's Tuesday," her mom breezed out the door as if that told Natalya anything.

Natalya was almost never in town on a Tuesday afternoon. The last time had been six months ago when Jessica had come home for her mother's fourth wedding to her father. On Tuesday they had…Natalya turned to her painting. Knitting in Eagle Cove was a twice-a-week affair. It felt a little odd as if she was about to step into her own painting. On her way out the door, she snagged the knitting bag her mother had thrown together since she hadn't brought her own.

They were halfway to town when her mom slowed the car.

Natalya looked up and saw someone walking toward them along the narrow lane. It was…

"Cal! Stop the car, Mom."

Her mother didn't. Instead she simply waved at Cal as they drove past him.

"Mom!" Natalya twisted in her car seat to see him looking after them in confusion.

"Don't worry. He'll still be around after knitting," and she drove on.

# # #

Cal watched the departing car as Natalya once again looked back at him.

She hadn't waved. Hadn't stopped.

Hard not to be disappointed, but she was going somewhere with her mother, and it wasn't out of town. Her MINI would still be out at the B&B. Still, he'd already walked a mile of the way out to see her.

Cal looked up at the sky. Horsetail clouds. Thin, wispy and still way up there, but weather coming. But when he looked out to sea, it was all clear—a rare crystalline blue sky descending right to the ocean without even a hint of sea mist.

Greg lived down this way with Jessica. He liked Greg well enough, but if Jessica was home, it would get awkward. Especially if the conversation turned to Natalya…which Cal guessed was who he wanted to talk *about* since he'd just lost his chance to talk *to* her. Harry wouldn't be back from his judicial duties in Newport until six. Alex was busy at out at Becky's brewery. And that's where Harry would be coming home to.

For lack of anything better to do, Cal turned and headed that way—a mile back to town and another out to the brewery. Becky was always good for a laugh, too. On his way back through town he'd raid tomorrow's day-old rack of some apricot Danishes he hadn't sold.

She and Natalya had been friends since forever and Becky was far less tricky than Jessica, especially when bribed with a Danish or two.

# # #

Natalya had abandoned the socks she'd started Friday night. She'd only started them because she could do socks in her sleep and it had kept her hands busy while everyone talked around her, mostly about Becky's honeymoon in Hawaii.

Instead of continuing the socks, Natalya had poked through the skeins in Becky's converted gun cabinet. She'd bought the glass-fronted mahogany piece for ten dollars from the fire hall's annual garage sale, when everyone in town exchanged their junk with each other and the rest went to Goodwill in the Valley. Natalya had walked right by it but with typical Beckyness, she'd seen more. Dusting it off and changing out the rifle rests for shelves, she'd made a beautiful yarn cabinet where Natalya had just seen garbage.

She stole a ball of honey-colored worsted weight and borrowed a set of number eight sixteen-inch cable needles. She'd also fished out a scrap of blueberry yarn that would be big enough to knit "Baker" in big letters across the front of the hat. She sat on a love seat next to Tiffany and cast on an extra six stitches for Cal's big head and started knitting.

Peggy arrived and she and Becky began comparing notes about the Judge and his son in overly happy tones. Andrea Martin complained about it as did May Conklin. Mrs. Winslow of course kept her own counsel on such matters.

Curiously, her mother didn't join in. Normally Gina Lamont would be at the center of teasing the two new brides for salacious details. She was listening, joining in, but she wasn't poking fun at them. Natalya was going to have to have a sit-down talk with her mom very soon. She'd been so wrapped up in her own world that she hadn't given much thought to anyone else's. But the middle of the knitting circle in Becky's living room wasn't the time or place, so she kept her questions to herself for now.

It wasn't as if she lacked questions of her own.

It was only after she was well started that Natalya wondered what it meant that she was knitting clothes for Cal. Okay, only a hat, and she'd knit them for boyfriends before. Or maybe, more accurately, she'd knit hats and sometimes mittens for lovers before. A lover was someone you had sex with. A boyfriend was more personal. Or had living in the city somehow screwed that up and gotten it backwards? A "lover" was supposed to be more important, but they'd somehow become less important. And boyfriend? Is that what Cal had become while she wasn't paying attention? Thinking of Cal as a "lover" was a whole diff—

Tiffany leaned over and looked at what Natalya had knit. On the relatively big needles the inch of knit-purl ribbing had gone quickly. She'd slowed down when she added in the second color to knit in the lettering and only had the bottom two rows so far.

"I don't think you're spelling it right," Tiffany said quietly. Other conversations continued among the knitters.

Natalya looked down but was fairly sure of her spacing. She'd done enough graphic design that she didn't need to map it out on graph paper for only five letters.

"You left out two of the dashes. Dash dot dash dot. Dot dash. Dot dash dot dot."

"What are you talking about?" The bottom tips of the five capital letters made a different pattern: dash, four dots, dash, and two dots.

"Morse code," Tiffany tipped her head sideways so that half of her face disappeared beneath her thick hair. "Sorry. I thought you were writing 'Cal' in Morse code."

"I—"

"If you went back and put in two more dashes, here and here," she pointed a slender finger, "you'd have it."

"I was spelling 'Baker.'" And wished she hadn't said it aloud because it made it too real. "In English."

"Oh," Tiffany nodded. "That makes sense then. In that case I think you need another stitch between the B and the A to get the spacing right."

Natalya considered and realized that the bulge of the B was going to end up too close to the A. She began ripping it out back to the ribbing, then stopped. She glanced at Tiffany who was back at work on a hat of her own—and intricate piece of Fair Isle knitting on number one size needles which meant it would be beautiful and take forever compared to her own number eights.

Tiffany had just assumed that Natalya was knitting for Cal. Did that make them a couple?

No, you've just been sleeping with him and having mad sex with him because he's a total stranger.

She really, really had to get her shit together.

She'd just managed to get the ribbing back on the needles without dropping any stitches when Tiffany spoke again.

"Now everyone will know."

"Know what?" But Natalya looked up. In the big double door that stood open between Becky's living room space and the microbrew tasting bar, stood a massive shadow. So big that it could only be Cal.

Out of the corner of her eye she could see her mother jolt in surprise and then sigh sadly. For an instant, she'd obviously thought it was Cal Sr. She and Mom definitely had to have a talk.

"Hello, Cal," Tiffany's raised voice slashed an abrupt silence across several overlapping conversations.

Everyone turned to look at her in shock. She'd never spoken so loudly.

Tiffany ignored them. She simply waved, then looked at Natalya.

"Get up, go over, and greet him," her voice was once again as soft as ever. "You know you want to," a barely audible whisper.

Natalya felt like a stick figure puppet as she stumbled to her feet. Someone, Tiffany, slipped the knitting out of her hands and gave her a little shove. She managed a stumbling step and now, with everyone watching her, she couldn't very well stop.

She crossed past the low coffee table covered in knitting patterns and tea mugs. Slipped by her mother *without* looking down at her. Exited the circle of knitters, briefly resting a hand on Mrs. Winslow's shoulder for balance, and came to a stop in front of Cal.

"Hey, Cal."

"Hey, Gnat," he looked as flummoxed as she felt.

Then he held aloft a white bakery bag.

"I brought apricot Danish."

\# \# \#

"Is it safe to come in?" Cal looked over her head at the circle of women watching him. All except Tiffany, who after shouting out a greeting was now quietly knitting again.

Natalya turned as if to survey the watching women before turning back. "Enter at your own risk."

"Mad dog in the yard, huh?"

"There is now," she teased and he felt better. He'd almost turned around when he saw all the cars. It had been weird that the brewery tasting bar was so busy on a Tuesday afternoon in January. But he'd already walked three miles to get here, then he saw Gina Lamont's car and poked his head in to investigate. The bar had been empty, so he'd followed the sound of voices.

Still, he hadn't anticipated walking in on an entire knitting circle. He'd planned to bribe Becky for information. Or guidance. Or something. Maybe even just hang out, have a beer, and catch up with Harry when he got home from playing judge.

"C'mon. You've entered the lion's den, might as well make a job of it." When Natalya reached out to take his hand, it was somehow the most natural thing to enter the circle.

The small couch that Natalya had been sitting on was empty. He was fairly sure Tiffany had been there, but now she sat on the far side of the group, looking as if she hadn't moved a muscle all afternoon.

Conversation was slow to restart, though when he remembered the bag of Danish, much to Becky's delight, it kicked back to life.

Unsure what to do next, he turned to Natalya. "What are you knitting?"

"Socks," she gasped out at him.

He didn't know much about knitting, but a glance around the circle revealed two or three people making socks and they were much smaller. Tiffany sat with her head tilted so far forward over her knitting that her long hair was practically a shield across her face. But it was shaking like she was laughing silently at some private joke.

"Damn big sock you've got there, Gnat."

"Wrong needles."

"Oh." But she wasn't doing anything about it either.

He looked up at the brewery tanks on the far side of the glass wall that divided Becky's odd living room from the works, wondering how long he could pull this off.

When he looked back down Natalya was bent over almost as far as Tiffany. The "sock" was gone and something much more sock-sized lay in her lap. She was being very careful not to look at him and Tiffany was still giggling to herself.

Cal settled back. Maybe this was going to be fun.

"How you doing, Ms. Lamont?"

Natalya's mom blushed bright red before answering.

Definitely fun.

# # #

"What kind of an idiot are you?" The instant Harry had entered the door, he dragged Cal away from the women and up the stairs.

"Smart as a whip, Slater. Comes from not hanging out with you for a decade."

"You can't just," he waved down the stairs, "just…those women are dangerous."

Cal leaned back in one of the big armchairs in Harry's upstairs office. "Nice place you've got here. Weird, but nice."

Becky had built herself a one room apartment in the barn's old hayloft. Kitchen, bed, bath, all in one space. She'd punched skylights out through the barn roof and placed a long line of windows which opened into the hayloft. When Harry had moved back, they'd extended it. He had a majestic oak desk, comfortable leather chairs, even a nice rug. It could have been a big city lawyer's office, if the view wasn't bales of hay stored just past the windows in one direction and the funky little Eagle Cove airport out the other windows.

"Mason. What the hell are you doing here anyway?"

Cal tipped his beer in Harry's direction. "That's a fair question, Judge."

"That's my dad," Harry complained.

"Get used to it, Judge. You're right, too confusing. Judge Harry, that works." Then Cal shifted trying to find a comfortable position in the big chair. "It's a question that I'm not quite sure how to answer. It has to do with Natalya."

"What about her?"

Okay, this wasn't going to be as easy as Cal had thought.

"Wait a minute," Harry thumped his beer down on the desk, planted his elbows, and leaned forward to glare across at Cal. "You and Natalya?"

Cal shrugged.

"Holy shit!"

"Yeah," Cal agreed.

"But she lives in Portland. You aren't moving to Portland, are you?"

"Wasn't planning on it."

"Well from what Jessica and Becky have said, she's kicking ass and taking names up there. Big promotion last fall, stuff like that."

"Shit!" It was worse than he'd thought.

"You and Natalya," Harry slumped back, taking his beer with him. "I'll be damned."

Yeah, that about covered it.

# # #

"Mom! Talk to me."

"Keep your voice down, honey."

"It's a car. There are two of us in it. Nobody cares if I can be overheard." And Natalya had gotten into her mother's car rather than going to find Cal because…she was a coward. Or maybe because she just wasn't ready to talk to him yet.

Sleep with him? Yes.

Relate to him? No.

Real nice, Lamont.

"What is it with you and Cal Sr.?"

"What is it with you and Cal Jr.?"

Natalya collapsed back in her seat. "I don't want to talk about it."

"There you go," her mother shrugged.

Natalya scrubbed at her face and did her best not to scream. After a series of deep breaths she didn't feel any better.

"It's your fault actually."

"*My* fault?" Natalya turned to look at her.

Uncharacteristically, her mother had both hands on the wheel and was staring straight ahead as if navigating Eagle Cove was impossibly challenging. Mom always talked with her hands, her contact with the steering wheel often marginal at best. And she always glanced over whenever they were talking. Now her normally expressive face was slightly clenched and aimed straight ahead.

"My fault?" Natalya forced her voice to remain calm.

"At the wedding. The way you two were dancing. I've known Cal Sr. my whole life. He was sweet on me in high school, but then all the boys were. And Tricia, she was something to see. Ended up, an idiot for kicking Cal to the curb and then abandoning her son, but still a total knockout," Mom shrugged. "Never really gave him any thought until I saw him standing as best man to the Judge and then the way you and Junior were dancing, I thought…why not."

"My fault," Natalya felt like a parrot repeating herself. "Is it serious?"

Again the shrug. "He's a fairly serious man. Hard to have casual sex with a man who makes everything seem so important."

Natalya considered that as they turned off Beach Way and onto LBB Lane. The road dipped and curved down toward the ocean. Then Natalya figured she should do her thinking aloud because her mother had been kind enough to break the deadlock.

"Cal, my Cal…not *my* Cal. Cal Jr." She had turned into a babbling idiot.

"See?" Her mother declared. "That's why I didn't want to talk about this. It's hard."

"Cal *Jr.*," Natalya tried again, "doesn't make things serious."

"So it's just casual sex?"

"It—" but the confirmation wouldn't come out. Someone you were having casual sex with didn't hold you silently all through a night. He didn't track you all over town and when he finally found you was content for an hour on the couch while joking with a circle of knitting women. She, and everyone else there, had been intensely aware of Cal's arm stretched comfortably along the back of the sofa, never quite touching her shoulders but commanding the space as if he ruled the world. It hadn't been possessive, at least it hadn't felt that way, he just…sat that way. So comfortable with his maleness. So at ease by her side.

"See?" Her mother prompted.

"I wish I didn't. If he's serious, then it gets insanely complicated."

"Uh-huh."

"At least you two live in the same town."

"Sure," her Mom practically snapped out. "I see him almost every day. And what happens when this falls apart and we still have to live in the same town? Tell me that one, Natalya."

Natalya stared over at her mother. She'd never heard her mom have so much emotion about a man. Not even That Unholy Disaster evoked such depth of feeling.

Her mom took the turn at the ocean and began driving up the long climb to the B&B.

"And what if it *doesn't* fall apart?" Natalya couldn't help asking. Once she said it, she didn't know if she was asking Mom about Cal Sr. or herself about Cal Jr.

Her mother drove in silence the rest of the way. When they were parked in the driveway, she still didn't move.

Natalya rested her hand over her mother's where it still clenched onto the steering wheel. She continued to stare out the windshield. When she spoke, it was so soft that Natalya could barely hear her.

"What do you think is scaring the crap out of me?"

Okay. That Natalya could relate to.

# # #

Cal didn't know what kept driving him.

Despite all of his plans, he couldn't quite ask Becky about Natalya. Even over dinner, he had kept the subjects on town news, the growth of both of their businesses caused by Jessica's effective promotions, and the upcoming Stormy Days event. They even cooked up a few new ideas that they could do to cross-promote more. Beer bread that he'd send her way with a supply of New York style giant pretzels for the tasting bar, and she had a spare display cooler that he'd install at the bakery to sell her wares by the bottle: beer and soda.

But not a word about Natalya until he and Harry were almost out the door. It was dark and the temperature rapidly dropping, so Harry had offered him a lift back to the bakery which he appreciated.

At the brewery's threshold, Becky had given him a surprisingly strong hug then whispered, "I can only wish for the two of you what Harry has given to me." Then she was gone and he was out in the wind.

Like it was serious between them or something.

Which maybe it was, because after Harry dropped him at the bakery and made sure they were on for poker Friday night, Cal hadn't gone upstairs. Instead, he'd climbed into the Corvette. Sometimes at night he'd take it for a spin up into the hills just for the fun of it—at night the road up to the pass was quiet and

Marty the town cop would long since be tucked in with his wife. Tonight he drove out to the B&B.

Halfway out he spotted Gina's car coming toward him. He pulled to the side as much as he dared without risking his paint job on the scrub salal, and rolled down his window. Seeing that, Gina stopped across from him and rolled down hers as well. The clouds were thickening up enough to make the moon a hazy patch in the otherwise blank night sky.

"Going to town?" Was the best he could manage.

She actually blushed a bit, which told him exactly where in town, then nodded. Then she said, "She's in her room. Just go on up."

Which had him doing the blush and nod in return. Uncomfortable with the moment, he offered his best smile. "Have fun, Ms. Lamont."

"You too, Cal," and for a brief moment her smile went huge.

By mutual consent, they rolled up their windows and drove off in opposite directions without another word.

He ran into a couple of guests trying to find decaf tea in the kitchen. He gave them a hand and then headed upstairs.

Asking to get hurt? Maybe.

Was Natalya worth the risk? Now there was the dumbest-ass question he'd ever asked himself in decades of stupid questions.

He knocked, and at her vague, "Uh-huh," swung open the door.

The image was a hard punch to the gut. Every light in the room was on, an additional pair of stand lights illuminating the canvas she worked on. He couldn't see it from this angle, sideways on, but Natalya in profile was stunning.

She had her hair back in a ponytail that exposed the fine lines of her features. She wore his baker's t-shirt, smeared and splotched with bits of color like a painter's smock. It had slid off her shoulder, one of the things he loved about the times Natalya wore his shirts, revealing a splendid expanse of her dusky skin. She was so intent that she didn't even turn to look at him.

"What is it, Mom?"

"Your mom isn't here."

Natalya didn't startle. She simply turned to look up at him for a long moment.

"I passed her on her way to Dad's."

"Oh," was all she said. Then after a long moment turned back to the canvas.

Well, if she wasn't going to be upset by it, he guessed that he wasn't either.

She continued with the painting almost as if she'd forgotten he was there. But he knew that wasn't the case; he could feel her attention tracking him even if her eyes weren't.

Not wanting to completely distract her, he began to circle the room, really looking at the art. Art never did much for him, but he could really see things in Natalya's works. Enough of Ma Slater's paintings had been displayed on the bakery walls for sale over the years that he recognized when a young Natalya had tried to imitate her. He could then see when she moved away from that and began developing her own style. By the time he'd reached the later paintings and sketches, he decided that he'd know her work anywhere. Not because he knew her so well, but because the voice of the images was so purely Natalya.

That's when he found the poker and knitting circle painting. It was something new, related, but new. Though the faces had been shifted, he knew every one of these people. Not Alex, Vincent, Harry, and Greg, but rather the younger, the softie, the joker, and the forthright. The women were equally distinctive. It took him a moment to see himself, so big in the foreground. It had to be him, she'd made his shoulders almost cartoon large. The peace of the woman watching him, seated in a different place, in a separate group, but not separate. The connection between.

Natalya came to stand close beside him, still holding palette and brush.

"You're breathtaking," and as he slid his hand around her waist and pulled her close he didn't know if he meant the woman in the painting, the painting itself, or Natalya as she tipped her head onto his shoulder. They remained that way for a long time, rocking gently.

"Make love to me, Cal." She whispered the request. Not "let's go to bed." Nor did she simply grab his hand and drag him over there. She leaned against him, perfectly still.

He disengaged the brush and palette from her clenched fingers and set them aside. Cal considered sweeping her up in his arms and crashing them down into the bed together. Or tossing her in the shower much as he'd tossed her in the ocean forever ago.

But she'd said, *Make love to me, Cal.*

So he did. When he pulled her close, Natalya ducked just enough to tuck her head under his chin, her nose brushing his collar bone. As they stood in the middle of the brilliantly lit room, he began giving her a standing backrub, working his fingers deep into tight muscles. Her body swayed against him as he applied pressure to particularly tight spots.

He soon had his hands under her t-shirt…his t-shirt, and her skin was so warm and soft against his palms that he simply stopped and held her tight for a long time. Her arms hung lifeless. But it wasn't as if she was unwilling, but rather unable to do more.

When he slid his oversized t-shirt off her slender frame, she didn't assist or protest, but leaned back into him as soon as it was out of the way. After he shed his own t-shirt, she turned just enough to lay her cheek on his shoulder, her arms slowly locking about his waist.

He'd never had a chance to study her, at least not under an artist's bright lights. Now he did, learning every curve that his hands had come to know so well. As he knelt before her, she wrapped her arms tight about his head, pressing his face into her belly.

For a moment, just a moment, he wondered what it would be like if a child was there, his child. It sent a shiver over his skin.

Would Natalya just leave, abandon her own child?

He looked up at her. Her head hung forward, her hair a loose shower framing her face as she swayed side to side, her smile so soft.

No. Not her. Natalya was not his mother. Natalya Lamont would be an incredible mother.

Something opened inside him. Like finding the surprise filling when opening a stuffed bread or biting down on a blueberry muffin only to find a strawberry jam center—which was a good idea, he'd have to remember that one.

He wasn't about to make love to Natalya Lamont.

He was about to do so with the one woman for him. She'd slid under his skin forever ago, playing her merry pranks on him. He now knew, beyond any doubt, that he had been the target and Harry was only caught in the by-blow because they'd been such buddies. Becky and Peggy's double wedding two weeks ago had only been the tipping point. It was as if all these years she'd been the only one for him and he was just now realizing it.

As he slid her pants off her lovely hips, he hoped to god it was true for both of them.

# # #

Sex had always been good. Even when it was bad, Natalya found that it was good in some way.

Never before had sex been devastating.

Of course she'd never asked anyone to make love to her before. And even if she had, which she hadn't, that person hadn't been Cal Mason.

She curled up against him as if she could somehow get closer than they'd already been. Cal had shattered her with his gentle mouth and strong hands. Then, with a frantic need previously unknown to her, she'd laid down right in the middle of the carpet and dragged at him until he was atop her and sliding inside until he had no more to give. She'd clung desperately, wrapping him tight in her arms and legs, as he drove them both into ecstasy.

When at last he'd collapsed onto her, she'd welcomed the weight, unwilling to let him go for even an instant.

Beyond words, they'd simply lain there beneath the bright lights clinging to each other. When they finally released one another, he'd swept her up in his powerful arms and carried her toward the bed, shutting off lights as he went. Now it was just the two of them and a small bedside reading light that he'd insisted stay on.

Still not speaking, he'd stroked and traced her eyebrows, cheeks, nose, lips, and chin as she clung to him. She'd felt as if she herself was being painted, cast into art, one fingertip stroke at a time.

What if it doesn't fall apart?

Then Natalya decided that her mother's fear was right

What if this is real?

Chapter 12

Cal woke in his favorite place, with his face planted between Natalya's breasts and her arms wrapped around his head. They were amazing breasts, as he'd taken great opportunity to study last night, but that wasn't it anymore. It was the intimacy of his nose pressed against the center of her chest. She smelled warm and ocean clean. She smelled of sex but she also, somehow, smelled of passion. Of heart.

She had given herself completely to him last night. It had been intimate but it had also been true. There was no longer any denying what there was between them. He needed her even more than he needed to bake. Besides, he didn't have to be in Eagle Cove to bake. There were bakeries in Portland, good ones, places he wouldn't mind working…if they weren't in Portland.

"Hey, Natalya."

"Hey yourself, Cal." She didn't protest about his using her proper name. She was no longer an annoying Gnat. She was his Natalya.

He'd been thinking of saying that he'd come visit her in Portland and check out some of the bakeries up there. He didn't want to, but he wanted her more. However, he changed his mind at the sound of her voice so thick with memories of last night. Definitely not the time to bring up any harsh realities. Instead he planted a firm kiss in the center of her chest and pulled back to look at her eyes.

Last night he'd never managed to reach the bedroom light on her side of the bed, as she'd fallen asleep wrapped about him and he'd been unwilling to disturb her. Now it let him see her eyes.

Her voice might be thick with soft memories, but her dark eyes were wary, glancing aside to avoid hard questions. Three-thirty in the morning didn't seem to be the time for confronting anything serious, so he kissed her on the tip of her nose and pulled her head down against his shoulder.

She nuzzled in against his shoulder and he enjoyed the sensations as her body slowly came awake against his. She slid completely beneath the covers, leaving him to look at the room as she roamed a line of kisses across his chest, her smooth hair sliding behind as if its passage permanently implanted the memory of each brush of her lips.

As he looked at the walls, he had the start of an idea.

It was crazy, but maybe it had some merit. Just maybe it—

She slid her lips and hands lower down his body and the thought skittered aside.

He took a deep breath and repeated his idea three times quickly to himself to make sure he had it firmly in mind. Then he gave his full attention to the delightful torture that Natalya was giving him beneath the covers.

# # #

"You want what?" Natalya wasn't really paying attention to Cal's words. Watching him dress beside her bed had her attention quite well occupied.

"Some of your paintings. We haven't had any good art on the wall of the bakery since Ma Slater died and everything was bought out. I'd like to put up some of yours." Sliding up his jeans didn't decrease her distraction, instead it made her think about sliding them right back off.

"Uh-huh. Sure." She attempted to focus on his face, but he hadn't pulled on his turtleneck yet. Natalya was more than a little mesmerized by his left shoulder, right there was where she'd slept so peacefully. "What are we talking about?"

"I want to put up some of your stuff for sale. Good for the bakery's look. Good for you if anything sells."

"Uh, okay. I guess. Sounds stupid to me, but if you think you can get anything for them, go for it."

"Thanks," he pulled down his turtleneck and shrugged on his jacket before turning to the paintings.

"Hey!"

He looked back at her, then smiled down. In two steps he had her pinned down, a hard kiss driving her back into the pillow and a none too gentle hand clamped onto her breast through the thick covers. Neither was quite hard enough to hurt, but both clearly demonstrated that last night had only heightened his need for her.

As quickly as he'd begun, he let her go, leaving her gasping for breath.

"A man's gotta bake."

"And birds gotta fly," she murmured because she couldn't think of anything more sensible to say with the heat he'd rekindled in her body. Rekindled hell. If she'd had any control of her muscles she'd jump him right now.

He grabbed three paintings, seemingly at random, then glanced at her as he stopped in front of *Joy*.

She shrugged. It was the painting of it that mattered to her, not the owning afterward. But it wasn't a wholly comfortable feeling.

"Don't just give that one away."

He nodded and picked it up, "I promise that I won't."

Then he was gone.

The bare spots on the wall bothered her.

But not as much as the painting that she'd carefully covered while Cal had prowled the room last night. His inspection had made her feel both terribly exposed and immensely appreciated. Her awareness of him had grown until he'd consumed more than her thoughts or emotions. Somehow, she'd needed to feel she was a part of him and he was a part of her.

And that's exactly what he'd done. Deeper than thought, deeper than her heart, they were a part of each other.

She'd been able to see it in Cal's eyes this morning. Knew he was going to say something stupid.

I'll give up Eagle Cove and Blackbird Bakery for you. It had been there, so clear just below the surface. It was a truth and a lie. She didn't doubt that he would, and she didn't doubt that it would kill his heart to do so. Even if he didn't realize it, she did.

How had they become so important to each other?

That jolted her from the bed and had her moving back to her canvas. She looked at the storm-torn seascape for a long time before reaching for her palette knife. Then she began methodically scraping everything she'd done off half of the painting.

Chapter 13

*W*ednesday *and Thursday passed* in chaos. And Friday wasn't starting out much different. There was a line in front of the bakery when Cal had returned from breakfast and the diner itself had been hopping.

Jessica hadn't put all of the events in the actual weekend. She planted teasers for several days before the Friday night kickoff to Stormy Days at Eagle Cove and man oh man were they working. The town had started filling up on Tuesday and was packed by Thursday night. The weekenders were in their houses days ahead. Vacation rentals were maxed out. The Sleepy Owl Hotel had its No Vacancy sign lit and the Lamont's B&B was booked out as well, including Natalya's room.

He'd offered Natalya his second bedroom as a studio, mostly filled with sporting gear he no longer used. No time to put it up for sale, he piled it to the side and she'd moved in there. Perhaps moved in was too strong a word—just an easel, her paints, and the one canvas that she wouldn't show him—but it changed everything. It had been his until his dad had given him the apartment and moved out, but he didn't tell her that in case it made her uncomfortable. Personally, he liked having Natalya working in his old bedroom.

At night, they'd crash into bed together, too exhausted to do more than cuddle. But they rose together and she'd go and close herself in that back bedroom.

Living together.

He'd never done that before. Some clothes and a toothbrush at each other's place, sure. Even the suitcase on the chair wasn't all that unusual when he'd dated the occasional tourist. But that one slender, hidden canvas made it so much more. Though it wasn't as if he saw much more of her than if they were living apart. Friday knitting and Friday poker were cancelled as the town hit capacity and struggled to keep up.

The Flicker movie house was running a winter film festival, without one Christmas movie among them. *Perfect Storm, The Eiger Sanction, Cliffhanger, The Ice Storm, The Day After Tomorrow,* and a list of others. Twenty-four hours of films running in a different order each day. You could either show up for a full day or purchase a time slot or two across successive days.

After eating at Carrier Pigeon Pizza, he'd gone back into their kitchen and tossed pizzas for them for an hour or two to help them catch up.

Cal barely had a chance to breathe. Dad stopped making excuses and simply showed up to help with the early morning prep, and they both stayed late.

"Gonna break your streak, Dad?" Cal didn't look up as he rolled out rye dough into a long thick snake on the floured marble block.

"Be damned if I know, Junior." His dad was doing the detail work of rolling up croissants: plain, chocolate, and almond. He was better at the fine pastries while Cal liked forming the larger breads and baguettes. Though custard fruit tarts were a lot of fun and he enjoyed doing those when they were in season.

Cal began chopping his dough snake into three-inch chunks. He rolled each into a fat ellipse and dropped it on a Silpat-lined baking sheet. They'd have to rise another half hour and then they'd bake up as hearty sandwich rolls.

"They're certainly defining new levels of confusion," his dad finished sheeting the croissants and shifted over to apple crisps.

Cal hadn't considered that. "You think it's a Lamont woman thing?"

His dad shrugged uncomfortably.

"Well, that would explain some stuff, wouldn't it?" Cal took a break long enough to slug back a mug of orange juice. Between the big ovens and intense work pace, he was sweating it out faster than he could drink it.

"It would," his dad stuck with water.

"So if it's just Lamont women—"

"We're both either lucky as hell or totally screwed and I'll be damned if I know which."

Cal didn't know either, so he pulled the sourdough out of the proofer and began setting the loaves up for baking.

But he was leaning toward lucky as hell.

Chapter 14

The storm slammed into Eagle Cove on Saturday morning. Thankfully it wasn't a Pineapple Express, like the one that had lashed the coast during Becky's wedding. Those storms were unrelentingly wet on top of the major wind blasts. Instead, this one was curling up the California coast where all of the worst windstorms came from. The powerful blasts ripped huge waves out of the ocean as it hammered the coast.

The drama was incredible, but by some miracle the power lines were holding up and the rain wasn't heavy enough to drive the tourists away. Instead, they ducked out for a few awestruck minutes watching the thirty- and forty-foot waves crashing down on the closed beaches, then scuttling inside. Which was right where the merchants wanted them.

Natalya had watched it all happening outside her win—Cal's window. The second bedroom that she was using as a studio was on the north side of the building and offered her a view up Beach Way, past the Puffin Diner, out to the breakwater. Eagle Bay had been formed by a narrow rocky spine that had resisted the Eagle

River's efforts to move it out to sea. On the inside was a small dockyard where a half-dozen fishing and tour boats huddled. On the outside, waves were slamming into it and shooting up high enough to see over Grouse Hardware's roof.

She didn't even look at the painting.

It was done.

Out in the living room, Cal had an incredibly tacky poster over the couch of a husky dog carrying a six of beer in its jaws. It was curling with age. It was easy to see that Cal didn't really live here. He slept here, but he lived for the bakery.

During the two days they'd holed up in the apartment together last weekend, she'd gotten the impression that they'd used the living room more in two days than he had in any two months prior. A comfortable chair and a TV were all he typically bothered with.

Neither the apartment nor his living room was hers to change—no matter how much it needed it—but she took the risk that he might like her painting more than the husky. The poster was so old that it cracked and split as she took it down. If he really loved it, she'd paint him a new one.

In its place, she hung the painting.

Again, she couldn't bring herself to look at it.

She cleaned up, changed, and slipped out of the apartment.

At the bottom of the stairs she detoured briefly into the bakery. It was, she checked her watch, two o'clock. Closing time, but they were packed. Cal Senior was working the counter; her Cal was in the open kitchen making sandwiches.

She slipped into the kitchen side of it.

"You doing okay?"

Cal looked at her a little wild-eyed, then grinned hugely. "Am now!"

She went up on her toes and gave him a quick kiss not wanting to slow him down.

He went back to his sandwiches, "You look pretty wrung out yourself."

"Flatterer."

"Is it working?"

"No, I really am wrung out. I finished the painting."

"Really, that's great. Do I get to see it now?" He made it a pout which was cute enough on a six-foot-four baker to make her smile.

"Sure. Upstairs, whenever you want. I'm gonna go home."

Cal froze and turned slowly to look at her.

"Just to help mom. I'm sure she's slammed too."

"But you'll be back tonight?" His whisper was desperate, barely louder than the hubbub of the packed bakery.

She nodded. He was so sweet about it, a nod was all she could do. She wanted to wrap herself around him and just hold on until the storm abated: the one outside, the one in her chest, and the one on the painting.

"Okay."

She waved and was halfway to the door when he called out to her.

"Oh you were right. I screwed up."

"How?"

"I underpriced your paintings."

"That's okay. It doesn't really matter. You actually sold some?" She hadn't expected that at all. She glanced out at the bakery walls but didn't see anything that was hers. Of course through the milling crowds it was hard to tell. There. The only one she could spot was *Joy*.

"Yeah," Cal came up to her and looked in the direction she was facing. "I told them that they couldn't take that one until tomorrow night. After the Stormy Days Festival is done."

"That one too?" Natalya had told Cal she was done with that painting, but maybe it wasn't done with her.

"We always had a deal with Ma Slater, one third-two thirds."

Sounded good to Natalya. Even at crappy prices it was the first time she'd ever sold her own art.

"Okay if we cut you a check on Monday?"

"I was—" her throat went dry. "I was going to drive back to Portland tomorrow."

Cal opened his mouth to protest, but was decent enough to close it again and nod. "The storm is probably dropping snow in the passes. You'll want to do that in daylight." His voice came out rough, almost hard.

"I don't want to leave either, Cal. You've got to get back to work. We'll talk tonight."

"Okay," he nodded to himself as if trying to gather energy. "Okay. And I'll cut the check for you tonight. Two grand."

"You joker," she went on her toes to kiss him again and headed out the door.

# # #

Cal watched her go. Watched his heart walking out the door. She waved, and was gone.

He went back and finished the latest sandwich order and delivered it to his father.

Something was itching. Something he didn't like.

"Dad, I'll be back in a minute."

"Don't have time for that right now, Junior." It was a tease, an actual tease from his dad.

"She's just gone out to help her mom."

"Oh. Okay. Did you tell her to say hello for me? Haven't had as much time as I'd like to pay attention to Gina this week."

Cal clapped his hand on his dad's shoulder in reassurance. After all, *they* both lived here and had all the time in the world. Natalya lived three hours away.

"Gonna take your damned minute anytime soon?"

"Oh, right," and Cal raced up the stairs to the apartment. He turned sharply for the second bedroom, but it was clean. Pristine. The easel had been folded. The paints and brushes tucked back into their small wooden case. The only sign of Natalya being here for the last five days was the dissipating odor of turpentine.

He stepped back into the living room and ground to a halt.

The stupid beer-toting husky that Harry had slapped up there in high school was gone. In its place hung what could only be Natalya's painting.

It was a self portrait.

Actually, it was many self portraits.

The background started as a murky, dark storm on the left. Slowly, agonizingly, it clawed and fought but was ultimately driven back by a lightening to the right. A tiny patch of blue sky, not quite at the top of the painting, but continuing off the right edge, promised hope and sunlight after the storm.

But that was the background.

Across the foreground was a woman. Repeated over and over. The leftmost figure, as tattered by the storm as the violent surf, looked to be on the verge of losing all hope. Survival was only a glimmer of a chance. Nothing more.

But as her repeated image moved across the storm, slowly crossing toward the viewer as she proceeded to the right, she became more and more well realized. More and more alive. And the rightmost figure looked out of the painting much as Natalya's self portrait had looked out of *Joy*. He almost hadn't put *Joy* up for sale because he didn't want to lose that image, but here it was again. Clearer, more fully detailed.

There was space for one more figure, but there wasn't…

But there was.

Faint within the clearing sky. Barely visible. The hint of a woman, not a full figure like the others, but just of the face. And the more he looked at it, the more clearly he saw her. It wasn't some suggestion of Natalya—it *was* her.

And she was smiling. Smiling at him with love in her eyes.

He stumbled back downstairs.

"Damn long one minute, Junior. I'm buying you a watch."

Cal blinked.

The crowds were still going strong but he couldn't really hear them over the ringing in his ears.

"Sorry, Dad. I just found out I'm going to marry Natalya."

His dad stopped and turned, right in the middle of taking an order. "She know that yet?"

Cal could only shake his head. "Doesn't make it any less true."

"Damn it!" His father scowled, but not at him. Maybe he wasn't the only one making a leap.

"Like son. Like father?"

His father realigned his scowl at Cal. "Just go make me three roast beef, two turkey, one with extra cranberry sauce, and a goddamned ham and Swiss sub with double meat and extra mustard."

"Sure thing, Pops." Cal felt like dancing as he returned to his station.

Dancing.

Maybe soon there would be another wedding to dance at with Natalya. Their own.

It just had to happen.

# # #

At the low point of LBB Lane where it dipped down to the beach, the cars were parked so thickly to either side that Natalya could barely sneak her MINI through the gaps. It was worse than July 4th. And then she saw why.

Vincent McCall wore his volunteer fireman's gear as he stood before an orange cone barrier strung with "Do Not Cross" tape and a "Beach Closed" sign. A hundred or more people in parkas and slickers were huddled together for support as seventy mile-an-hour blasts tried to knock them off their feet.

And beyond them, the tide was coming in.

This stretch of the coast always had five- to six-foot breakers. Storms kicked that up into the ten- to twenty-foot range. These monsters were running consistently at the high end of that range with a few even bigger. When they landed she could feel her car shake in the heavy thunder.

A tree stump the size of a small RV was being tossed about by the pounding surf. Forty-foot logs, long since stripped of all branches and bark didn't just roll, they tumbled.

Everyone had a camera out. Which they were going to find to be a very costly mistake. The spray, sheeting landward with the wind, would be thick with corrosive salt water. Even by coastal standards this was a big one. What the tourists didn't know was that Monday, after the storm had passed, that's when the truly monstrous waves would come crashing in.

She spotted Jessica wearing a huge grin.

Yes, this was a Stormy Days at Eagle Cove that would be talked about for years to come. The one that all future festivals would be measured against.

Natalya waved, wasn't seen, but it didn't matter. She continued to the B&B.

Her mother was out, but everything was in order. There were even little lemon custard tarts and Murchie's tea set out in the parlor for teatime.

There were guests staying in Natalya's room, so she headed for her mother's. It was actually a cozy suite of three rooms on the second floor with its own balcony. Instead of the powerful-women theme that defined the rest of the B&B's rooms, her suite was like the parlor: cozy elegance. It had been the private quarters of the daughter of the town's founder and Natalya's own mother had preserved it in its original form.

A living room big enough for entertaining six but not eight had a large fireplace, a tiny kitchenette, and a sweeping view of the coast and ocean for miles to the north and west. The bedroom to the north side was an aerie in the trees, looking toward the state forest. Her mother had made it into a comfortable office from which she conducted the B&B's business. But it was also a library of books and movies with a moderate-sized screen hidden tastefully in a mahogany armoire.

Natalya went into the master bedroom and sat on the quilt—an elegant heirloom piece in dusky reds and deep golds.

The private balcony was accessible only from here. And it faced due west into the storm.

She watched it shred the waves for a long time.

172

Chapter 15

C*al looked at his* father slumped across the table from him. They were in the back corner of the Brass Plover, nursing a burger and a beer. It was packed to the limits, but May had found a spot for them close by the kitchen.

"Tomorrow's got to be easier."

"Sunday," Cal agreed with a groan. "Tourists leave early on a Sunday."

"Why were we greedy enough to stay open on a Sunday?"

"Wasn't greed," Cal shook his head.

His father eyed him as he sipped his beer.

"Okay. It wasn't just greed. Did you want to be the one to tell Jessica no?"

Senior didn't have to consider before shaking his head no.

"I got a new side business."

That got his father's full attention. His father had never thought much beyond baked goods, but Cal was always adding new ideas and the bank balance growth had convinced his father to start doing the same. They were almost big enough to buy out the Plover when May decided to retire. Side by side eating establishments; they'd make good.

"Put up some of Natalya's art."

"Uh-huh."

"Sold it."

His father just watched him.

"All of it. All that she gave me."

That earned him one of his father's rare smiles. "Seems I remember something about your grandpa doing the same for Ma Slater. Gave her a start back when she was younger than you and the Judge was courting her."

"That's where I got the idea."

His father held up his beer in a toast. "Guess I didn't raise no fool."

"Nor did Grandpa," Cal toasted him back.

They both drank deep and set their glasses down in unison.

"Now about these women…" his father started up again after finishing his fries.

"Yeah," Cal couldn't agree more.

"Yours come back yet?"

"Not that I've seen." And Cal had been sitting where he could just see his apartment out the window. Not a single light had come on.

"Haven't seen much of Gina either."

"Nope," Cal agreed.

"Guess we oughta go find them."

"Make sure they're okay," Cal nodded. "What with the storm and all."

His father just snorted. "You ever met two more capable women?"

"Hey," Cal protested as he polished off the last of his beer and stood. "I just need an excuse, not a reason."

His father actually laughed, then slapped him on the shoulder to lead the way.

# # #

"I found her in here. Graceful as ever."

Natalya was vaguely aware of someone speaking. She cracked open one eyelid and saw her mother silhouetted in the doorway, with two faces looking over her shoulders. Two men. It was—

Someone flipped on the bedroom light.

Natalya yelped and covered her eyes but it was too late, the image of Cal's evil grin was seared into her retina.

It took her a moment to get oriented. It was evening, darkness had fallen and the storm still raged against the glass doors to the balcony. Her mother's bed. She'd fallen asleep; didn't even remember curling up and hauling a corner of the quilt over herself.

When she dared squint her eyes open again, her mother and Cal Sr. were gone, but Cal Jr. still leaned lazily against the door jamb.

"Get out. Just give me a minute."

"Sure thing, Gnat," he flicked off the light and closed the door.

"Jerk."

They were all sitting in the suite's living room by the time she staggered out, still half asleep and squinting against the brightness. She went to the small fridge in her mother's kitchenette. She found a bottle of pear juice and a piece of cold fried chicken. She sniffed it. Her mom's homemade. Major score! A plate and a paper towel and she was set.

She joined the others in the living room, but sat on the armchair beside her mom rather than on the couch by Cal. Natalya needed a little distance from him. Something more than inches. A whole afternoon worrying at the problem of her being stuck in Portland had served nothing except to wear her into exhaustion.

Reaching out, she took her mom's hand.

"Eww! Greasy!" Her mom yanked her hand away. "Use the towel first."

"Sorry," Natalya wiped her hand, but returned to eating. The problem was, everyone else focused on her eating as well.

"Talk about something," she waved a hand at them.

"Okay," Cal Senior spoke carefully. "Let's talk about long-term plans."

Natalya glanced at her mother, but she didn't know what was going on either. Then her eyes widened just as Natalya's own suspicions kicked in.

"No!" She blurted out, spraying flaky fried chicken crumbs all over her lap. "No. We're not talking about that."

"Oh, but we are," Cal agreed with his father. He slumped down on the couch, lacing his fingers behind his head and looking ever so relaxed.

"I'm listening," her mother said softly.

"You're what?" Natalya slapped a hand over her mouth as a few more bits of crust came out. "Sorry," she mumbled through her fingers. "Didn't mean to shout." She sipped some pear juice and swallowed to make sure she'd swallowed it all.

"At least *I* am," her mother replied. "I at least want to hear what they're thinking."

"There isn't a *they*. There can't be a *they*. The world doesn't work like that."

The two Cals watched her through narrowed eyes, then looked at each other. Whatever silent father-and-son conversation was going on, it had them both grinning.

"Besides," Natalya already knew the answer. She hated it, but could find no other. "My answer would have to be 'no.' So please don't ask."

At least Cal stopped looking so damned relaxed, but his father didn't even bat an eye.

"You got something against Eagle Cove, girl?" Senior made it sound like a crime.

"God no! I love it here. My mom," Natalya wiped both of her hands on the paper towel and then reached out to take her mom's hand, who inspected it briefly before accepting the handclasp. "My mom is here and I miss her. Why do you think I come back so much? But my job is in Portland."

"Pretty attached to that job?"

"What is this? The Spanish Inquisition?"

"Comfy chair next," Cal agreed, but his father's glance quelled him before he could continue the old Monty Python routine.

"Pretty attached to that job?" Senior asked again.

"I'm most certainly attached to the paycheck."

Cal Sr. nodded thoughtfully. "Can't do it from here? Remote… whatever they call it?"

"Telecommuting and distributed teams. Not really. Don't even want to do it much anymore, but they pay me really well."

For reasons beyond her Cal brightened up, but his father hushed him.

"Junior tells me he sold some of your paintings."

"You sold some paintings?" Her mother practically cried out. "Why didn't you tell me?"

"He did it," she waved a hand at Cal. "Just told me this afternoon, so there's no way I could have told you sooner. He sold *Joy* as well."

"Oh, I liked that one."

"It's okay, Ms. Lamont," Cal leaned forward. "Wait until you see the one she replaced it with."

"Did you like it?" Natalya really hoped Cal had liked it. She'd tried to put everything she couldn't say "yes" to into it so that he'd at least have that much of her.

"I'll never take it off that wall unless we move somewhere else."

"Crap!" Natalya dragged a free hand through her hair, the one she hadn't wiped off.

Ick!

"Cal, I just said there isn't a we. There can't be. And no, you can't leave your bakery. Your heart would die out there in the world."

Again he leaned back in that arrogantly male way of his, his smile utterly denying the truth.

"I did mention that I sold some of your paintings," he repeated himself.

"Sure," Natalya waved a dismissive hand. "Then teased me with some ridiculous number not even worthy of comment. If you're going to make a joke work, you have to at least make it believable."

If Cal's grin got much bigger he'd have pear juice in his hair and the remains of a greasy chicken down his shorts.

"What if I told you it wasn't a ridiculous number?"

"How much was it?" Her mother asked in a whisper.

"But you said it was underpriced."

"Uh-huh!" Cal slouched back even more. "I bet I could have gotten half again for *Joy*."

"What was the number?"

But Natalya couldn't even speak to answer her mother's question.

"Three thousand," Cal Sr. said.

"But you said 'two thousand,'" she accused Cal Jr., finding her voice.

He nodded, "Bakery keeps a third as commission. That's two thousand to you. I'd wager you could make a better living with your art here in Eagle Cove that doing web stuff in Portland."

Natalya didn't know what to say. The idea was too big. Too close to dreams she'd never dared have. Never shared with anyone…including herself. Yet, like some miracle, Cal had found them.

"Now?" Cal asked his dad.

Cal Sr. gave a judicious nod.

Then they both rose and came to stand in front of their chairs: Cal Sr. in front of her mom, Cal Jr. in front of hers.

Her mother squawked as the two men knelt.

Natalya couldn't even manage that.

"Of course," Cal spoke ever so softly. "There is a way to keep *all* that money in the family."

Natalya looked over at her mother, just as her mother turned from looking at Cal Sr. while he knelt before her. Her eyes were glowing with joy. True joy.

The men, in turn, grinned at each other before speaking.

"Do you two ladies—" Cal Sr.

"—like double weddings?" Cal Jr.

Natalya shared a smile with her mom, then they turned back to face their men before speaking in unison.

"We do."

About the Author

M. *L. Buchman has* over 40 novels in print. His military romantic suspense books have been named Barnes & Noble and NPR "Top 5 of the Year," nominated for the Reviewer's Choice Award for "Top 10 Romantic Suspense of 2014" by RT Book Reviews, and twice Booklist "Top 10 of the Year" placing two of his titles on their "The 101 Best Romance Novels of the Last 10 Years." In addition to romance, he also writes thrillers, fantasy, and science fiction.

In among his career as a corporate project manager he has: rebuilt and single-handed a fifty-foot sailboat, both flown and jumped out of airplanes, and designed and built two houses, Somewhere along the way he also bicycled solo around the world.

He is now making his living as a full-time writer on the Oregon Coast with his beloved wife. He is constantly amazed at what you can do with a degree in Geophysics. You may keep up with his writing by subscribing to his newsletter at:
www.mlbuchman.com.

Coming soon, Eagle Cove #4:

Keepsake for Eagle Cove
(excerpt)

Envying other people wasn't something Tiffany Mills had much experience with and she didn't like it. Especially not when they were hugging her so fiercely.

She'd always thought of Natalya Lamont as the calm and collected one of her friends. Well, not her friends, but Natalya's.

Maybe it was just her wedding that had her bubbling like a giddy schoolgirl.

Of course Natalya's mother also was exhibiting similar behavior as it had been her wedding day as well—a mother-daughter marrying a father-son event. But Gina Lamont was a generally more effusive type, so at least it was expected of her.

Tiffany wanted to ask what it felt like to be so happy, but resisted the urge. Delaying a bride making the rounds wouldn't be nice.

Natalya finally let her go, then gave her another quick hug before spinning back into the congratulatory crowd surging through and around the Lamont B&B. It was a gorgeous day for Eagle Cove, Oregon. The big Victorian overlooking the Pacific Ocean was packed with wedding revelers. The parlor and the kitchen overflowed out onto the porch on the warm May day. That was where Tiffany had retreated to, a small bench on the verandah that let her overlook the events on the lawn without getting snarled up in them.

Becky Billings had lobbied to have the event out at her brewery, and they would have moved it there if the weather hadn't cooperated. But it was a beautiful day. They'd planned the ceremony early enough that they could dance on the front lawn overlooking the ocean during the warm afternoon before the cool spring evening chased everyone inside. They'd wanted to be wed in the family home, the last house before the big headland that defined the end of Eagle Cove.

Tiffany wondered how remote that made her: living solo, clearing the forest and homesteading a full mile more into the hills. Far from town. She'd found a small gap between two plat surveys of adjacent state forests and, much to the Oregon Department of Forestry's surprise, had purchased the ten-acre error from the state. She was in "unincorporated" forest—technically she wasn't even in a county. Maybe she should declare her *own* county, or better yet her own country. Occupancy of one human, fifty chickens unless some more eggs had hatched this morning, a dozen pigs, and an exceptionally lazy cat the color of an orca whale (black with a white belly) and roughly the same blobbish shape who kept Tiffany's lap warm on cold nights. The cat only roused herself for mouse hunting—at which she excelled.

Oregon State law had some considerations that might make it implausible to declare independence and Federal law definitely did. Maybe she could declare her own state. Of course then she'd have to decide whether or not to sign onto the Interstate Commerce Commission for fair trade with other states, perhaps even elect a governor. Of course, with only one resident, the choice would be obvious and the balloting easy.

Tiffany raised her right hand, "And the ayes have it."

"Good. They can keep it," Jessica Baxter slapped her hand like a high-five then eased herself down onto the bench beside Tiffany. "If my husband ever tries to touch me again, he's going to get a big-ass nay."

"You're huge!" At eight months pregnant Jessica seemed to be expanding daily.

"Tell me something I don't know." Jessica had been the first of Natalya's friends to get married. And every one of those eight months showed on her belly. She was five-ten—Tiffany wouldn't have minded the extra four inches—and slender as could be, except for the pregnancy. From the back she looked perfectly normal as she had one of those pregnancies that went straight forward.

"You probably don't know why your five times great-grand-mother never spoke to her daughter." And then Tiffany wished she could cut her tongue out.

Jessica blinked at her in surprise.

Tiffany could only hope that it would be written off as *just one of those "things" that Tiffany Mills says.*

"Wait," Jessica furrowed her brow as she massaged her back. "Five times…you're talking about the founders of Eagle Cove."

Tiffany really didn't do well with people.

Jessica, she knew, was tenacious and now that she'd latched onto it, wouldn't let go. Tiffany didn't want to reveal how she knew what she did. She suspected that her normal ploy of shaking her hair forward and "going shy" while focusing on her knitting wasn't going to work this time. Especially as she hadn't brought her knitting.

"Hi."

Tiffany looked up at the man now standing eye-level to them, two steps down from the porch. He was lean and had brown eyes beneath tousled hair of the same color. He wasn't dressed like a wedding guest, but rather in unseasonably early shorts, a plain t-shirt, and hiking boots. She glanced around but saw no sign of a pack.

"I don't want to crash the party, but I think I'm in the right place. This is the Lamont B&B?" He looked around a little lost, a feeling that Tiffany knew well.

Grabbing any distraction she could, Tiffany rose to face him as he climbed the last two steps. He was only a few inches taller than she was. "It is. It's also the Lamonts' weddings, both of them."

"Oh, that explains it. Maybe I'll, uh, just come back in a few days."

"Did you have a reservation?" Tiffany almost grabbed his arm as he started to turn away. Jessica hadn't moved from the porch seat close behind her.

"No. Not really. And not yet. I'm a couple days early. Once I got in my truck…" he shrugged, "I just drove."

"I think the B&B's full with wedding guests, but let's go check." Tiffany took his hand and led him inside. At the last second she risked a glance at Jessica, and saw that she hadn't gotten away with anything.

# # #

Devin Robison had rarely felt so out of place in his life. He'd slept in the back of his pickup last night in the Boise National Forest. Up with the sun, he'd landed in Eagle Cove nine hours later in the middle of a wedding. It was terribly disorienting, and not just the road weariness meets wedding scenario.

He'd thought that growing up in Chicago had prepared him for great expanses of water. Lake Michigan was Chicago's front yard—three hundred miles long and a hundred wide. But when he'd broken out of the Coast Range forest before the final descent into town and seen the entire Pacific Ocean before him, he'd nearly crashed his Toyota in surprise. Unless you happened to stumble on an island, Tokyo was five thousand miles away, which was on an island anyway. The expanse was impossible to comprehend.

Neither Chicago nor the towns he'd driven through in the last four days had prepared him for the tiny size of Eagle Cove. A mile from forest to ocean and two miles along the beach…and it wasn't densely populated. The next town of any size was thirty miles up the coast. He'd been on the verge of turning around from an attack of agoraphobia, the fear of open spaces—or maybe just plain nerves. He hadn't realized that such obscure places even existed. Eagle Cove was so remote, so wild.

He'd been looking for a fresh start, had needed one desperately, but he'd left "middle America" somewhere staggeringly far behind.

Finding the massive Victorian home had been easy. "Find LBB Lane at the far end of downtown," which was a grandiose term for a business district four blocks long. "Go to the end of the road."

Then he'd seen the gorgeous house. It was exactly the sort of structure that had led him into architecture school. Three stories of classic, early 1880 American Queen Anne Victorian. He'd fallen in love the moment he'd seen it. The house was one of the best examples he'd ever seen of the style. Unlike so many of the ones in Chicago, the whimsy had not been allowed to overwhelm the beautiful lines and overall cohesiveness of the design. Yet it was still playful with circular turrets, balconies, and a wrap-around porch.

A wrap-around porch clogged with people.

Devin floated through a kitchen solid with people, anchored in this reality only by the hand of the woman leading him.

The woman leading him.

Few greeted her, though they readily moved aside, allowing her a straight line passage. His first sight of the kitchen had made him wonder if was even possible to cross. Yet for whoever-she-was, they moved aside. He was half tempted to guess that it was magic, as people almost didn't notice that they made way for her. They certainly didn't break their conversations for her passage.

He usually at least knew the name of someone he was holding hands with. Had there been introductions? He didn't think so. He'd been too busy trying to see her eyes beneath the wide brim of her felted hat. As he'd come up the steps, he'd seen twin glints of blue-gray. Between the big hat and the nearly waist-long fall of thick tawny hair that half covered her features, he'd been unable to confirm that first impression.

Her blouse and skirt were…rustic for lack of a better word. Perhaps bohemian, as the maroon belt made of a wrapping of fabric defined a trim waist and made her clothes look nice. Maybe someone's mild-mannered and carefully cloistered cousin. Except for her hands. The one holding his was firm, even if she didn't hold on hard, the strength of her fine fingers was obvious. And hard calluses. She worked with her hands a lot.

"What's your name?" They'd come to a small nook in the back corner of the kitchen. It felt oddly quiet here though he could hear a dozen different conversations. She let go of his hand to pull out a register. The woman spoke softly, but he could hear her despite the other noise.

"Devin. Devin Robison."

She didn't offer her own, but began flipping through the pages. Then she stopped as if shocked. She looked up at him sidelong.

Yes, more gray than blue, at least the one eye inspecting him.

"Who are you?"

Devin figured that if he could answer that one, he wouldn't be here. "Am I in the book?"

She nodded with a mesmerizing slide of long hair. "Yes."

"Is there a problem?"

This time the hair shimmered side to side.

"And?" What a curious person she was.

"Gina Lamont gave you the best room in the house other than her own. Until today it was her daughter Natalya's, though she's been living with her husband in town."

"I take it that's unusual."

She tipped her hat back enough that he could at least see her smile. "More than a little."

"Maybe we should check with her."

"Wedding day. I think she has enough distractions. Let me show you the way." She took a key from the hook and once again led him away, though without taking his hand this time. He kind of missed it.

He wanted to inspect the house as they went, but found himself unable to look away from the *still* nameless woman leading him up the twisting stairs and along a narrow hallway.

Available soon at fine retailers everywhere

Other works by M. L. Buchman:

Angelo's Hearth
Where Dreams are Born
Where Dreams Reside
Maria's Christmas Table
Where Dreams Unfold
Where Dreams Are Written

Eagle Cove
Return to Eagle Cove
Recipe for Eagle Cove
Longing for Eagle Cove

The Night Stalkers
Main Flight
The Night Is Mine
I Own the Dawn
Wait Until Dark
Take Over at Midnight
Light Up the Night
Bring On the Dusk
By Break of Day
White House Holiday
Daniel's Christmas
Frank's Independence Day
Peter's Christmas
Zachary's Christmas
Roy's Independence Day
and the Navy
Christmas at Steel Beach
Christmas at Peleliu Cove
5E
Target of the Heart
Target Lock on Love

Firehawks
Main Flight
Pure Heat
Full Blaze
Hot Point
Flash of Fire
Smokejumpers
Wildfire at Dawn
Wildfire at Larch Creek
Wildfire on the Skagit

Delta Force
Target Engaged
Heart Strike

Deities Anonymous
Cookbook from Hell: Reheated
Saviors 101

Dead Chef Thrillers
Swap Out!
One Chef!
Two Chef!

SF/F Titles
Nara
Monk's Maze